Enigma Books

Bernard Uzan

The Shattered Sky

A Novel

ENIGMA BOOKS

Published in the United States by
Enigma Books
580 Eighth Avenue, New York, NY 10018
www.enigmabooks.com

Translated from the French by Robert L. Miller

ISBN-10 1-929631-71-5
ISBN-13 978-1-929631-71-1
Cover design by: Robert Farrar-Wagner
Printed in the United States of America

Library of Congress CIP available upon request.

The Shattered Sky

Pariz

Paris in the early morning is one of the rare pleasures I truly enjoy. The alarm clock next to my bed rings at seven, and it's high time to go. The bathroom mirror reflects a picture I know only too well. My face is filled with anger and despair in its complete rejection of the entire world as it exists. I look at myself and I feel like crying.

I'm living in the Montparnasse section of Paris, in an apartment that I share with Nicolas. I push open the door on to the rue Vavin…

I follow my usual itinerary, and walk along the Luxembourg Gardens, down the rue Bonaparte, to Mabillon, and the Odéon… It's not easy to cross the street with all the traffic and the people who are hurrying early in the morning to reach their real jobs, with the very specific objective of getting to their office and doing as little work as possible…

Cars and pedestrians grind to a halt, and everything appears to be paralyzed…

A long black limousine goes by slowly, followed by many other cars with their parking lights blinking on their way to a funeral … this early in the morning, they must be in a hurry to bury the dead… a long line of cars for an important person no doubt. The big black car doesn't look at all like the old hearse they used to take my father away.

They've made some progress since then to bury you. It happened six years ago, and I was twenty-one, the age of reason… The whole family is waiting at the entrance of the hospital, they're all talking at the same time like a bunch of traders in an open air market. I keep quiet, I am silent, the blade of a knife sears my stomach, a hand is crushing my heart. Finally, after an unbearably long time, the hearse arrives…

The two funeral parlor attendants who load the casket into the hearse tell me to sit up front because of the heat. I'll be more comfortable up front…

"We'll be much more comfortable up front," repeats my uncle.

"Oh yes! We'll be more comfortable up front," adds my aunt.

"We'll be much better up front," insists my mother.

They all hurry, push and shove, to grab the best seats faster, faster, as the door is about to slam shut; a few flowers tumble out in the scuffle. I hear my father moaning, but no one else can hear him; they prefer to sit by the windows, and we're off.

The tall black van moves ahead, and I am sitting very comfortably on a soft black, feathery leather seat. The leather is as soft as a bed or soft like my father's eyelids when I closed his eyes on his hospital bed. Thrown on the floor among the rows of seats, almost between my legs, is a wooden box covered with many flowers, red flowers, blue, yellow, green and inside that box, a dead man...

My father.

It's three in the afternoon, my father died two days ago, my very own father, not my neighbor's father or the father of the guy who runs the corner store; no, this time it's my father, my very own father.

Two days! He must already look pretty bad!
I'm sitting alone with two seats to myself, at just about the location where my father's belly should be. The others are sitting two by two, yakking away. They must have so many interesting things to discuss. They are off on a picnic; if this goes on much longer they'll surely extract some food from their handbags, some dry sausage and red wine, no, it would probably be dry crackers.

The hearse is moving very slowly through the streets of Paris, clearly this is going to take a long time. They're bored; they shift around on the black cushions, blow their noses, exhale loudly, perspire, sigh, stretch out, and finally yawn, at last: it's so hot, so sticky. I begin to doze off; Paris always struck me as being a gluey, sticky city. A sticky city...

I only like Paris in the morning, very early, when only lost souls like myself are wandering around in search of what they are, what they used to be or what they will become....

The whores are finally ready to go to sleep, the garbage collectors are picking up the shame of humanity, college students have finally restructured the world after splitting pubic hairs all night long, and out of work actors, such as myself, think of themselves as Hamlet as they cross the Seine on the Alexander III Bridge…

I love Paris, especially on Sunday mornings when the neighborhood, where I spend most of my time, is totally deserted… the early morning, is both hot and cold, the silence is filled with noises. I hear the silence so clearly that it scares me…that silence… Within me silence descends regularly… I learned to keep so many things quiet for fear that they might make me explode. A fear that never lets go of me… The fear of being or of not having…

Paris is a sticky place for the underprivileged, the poor bastards, the out-of-towners, those who live in the suburbs, the out-of-work actors.

Tunis used to be sticky too, especially in the afternoons when during the summer months I am forced to take a three hour nap.… I love swimming in the green or blue sea so much, it's the only time I feel just like everybody else; when I can show off my strength and compete with my cousins; when I can make believe that I am a complete human being, just like any other. I swim and swim, I'm not afraid of the waves, and my arms are strong. Nobody can see my grotesque looking, lifeless legs that make the neighbors and the school children laugh… And I want to swim all day, all my life, without stopping. I swim far, very far from the water's edge and they call after me and wave their arms wildly and are worried. I'm happy and laugh out loud and ask everyone to look and admire me in the water. But no! I must take a nap everyday! I am thrown on my bed and forgotten like a pile of dirty laundry, full of unmentionable spots. I hate it. I hate taking a nap every day. They sleep or make believe they're sleeping while I'm bored to death.

I am dying of shame and boredom.

I hear the silence of the street, I hear the silence of the unbearable sun that crushes the senses... Over one hundred degrees in the shade in Tunis...where everyone is asleep, and it's two o'clock in the afternoon.

I grab a matchbox and amuse myself by setting fire to the ants that crawl along the walls of my bedroom, the bedroom of a crippled child. I like to burn them one by one. I can see their tiny, sticky bodies twisting desperately in the flames...The ants are screaming with pain and I burst out in laughter.... Hundreds of ants like the hundreds of Jews in Nazi Germany's meat grinders... The flames of the tiny matches are like the crematorium; I have the power. I can burn bodies with total impunity. The silence of the street is marked by the moaning of the ants and the calls of the street vendors...

"Ropa ve-ecchia!!!"

"Sharpen your knives, sharpen your scissors, the sharpener is here!

"Ices, Bobby's ices!"

"Jasmine flowers, jasmine flowers..."

I'm having a hard time burning them today. The ants are everywhere, in every corner of my room and it takes me such a long time to get from one corner to the other...

They're really oblivious about everything... They could have set my room up to suit my needs, my tasks... After all, I'm the only one who is in this condition... A bit of decency for the cripple, have some consideration for the polio stricken boy who can't walk without help.

5

Maybe some of the ants are also crippled by now; some of them must have lost their legs, or rather their feet...

I place some bread crumbs to attract more ants and......

Okay, well enough about the ants... That's all old stuff, ancient history, the time when I was nothing at all...on the way to becoming someone... Now I am... What am I? What? One of the living dead, a live one who is really dead and walking around Paris in search of time past... I think I'm Marcel Proust. But Proust should have called it *In Search of Times Dead*.

Dead, like my father.

They're back with their yakking and I open my eyes. Everybody is talking inside the hearse, my mother, my uncles, my aunts, everybody is complaining about the heat, except my father who says nothing, as usual.

It's true that it's really hot; my grandmother is sweating like a pig, like a big bloated woman in a bikini, on the beach sweating uncontrollably like a leaking pipe, her hat looks like a flowery beach cap; she is absolutely grotesque.

Paris on a Thursday at three in the afternoon; cars, trucks, traffic jams, red and green lights, delivery boys, hookers, cops, pimps, ambulances, and the cemetery that is still so far away. It's going to be a long ride. Thankfully we were all careful and sat by the windows.

"At least we'll be able to breathe." says my uncle

Opposite me, my aunt is crossing her legs, what magnificent tanned thighs; she's not wearing stockings because it's so hot...and me... I'm alone on my seat and I'm feeling even hotter; my father next to me must also feel very hot...the freshness of the wreaths and the flowers are no help when you're in a box where you can't breathe.

My aunt crosses and uncrosses her legs; she notices me looking at her and she hikes up to her thighs. She's staring at me and licks her lips, then slowly with her nails, she softly caresses her knees, rearranges her necklace over her breasts, looks at me and smiles; my father, who knows her very well, must also be smiling inside his box.

My uncle, two rows behind, tells his son a story and laughs, softly at first, then louder and louder as he holds his stomach. He is laughing loudly and uncontrollably to the point of tears; suddenly he realizes it's uncouth.

"It's because I'm nervous," he says, and then stops.

But his laughter catches on and I start laughing and laughing, my aunt's thighs are laughing, my teeth scratch my lips, my aunt's thighs are laughing out loud, my father is hurting in his box and has trouble breathing, his breath grows shorter, my aunt smiles showing her teeth, my uncle smiles, the people in the street and even those damn dogs are smiling. Tomorrow I'll go pay a visit to my aunt whose thighs are laughing and the mere thought makes me so excited that I have to pull my jacket down over my pants so they won't notice...everything is spinning, my head is pounding, I close my eyes...

"Come back, come back and set things straight, you have no right to go, nothing is right without you, nothing can be good, nothing can be straight, don't leave! Come back."

My mother's elbow wakes me up....

"Come on now! You don't doze off in a hearse especially when it's your own father who is dead, watch your manners! Who brought you up? Yes, I know it's hot but that's no excuse. If you partied less you wouldn't be falling asleep on the day of your father's funeral."

My mother plunges her face back into her handkerchief and dries her tears. I stop laughing, and I look out the window.

The street is still, the same as it was before and yet my father is dead. I don't get it.

"Switch seats with me," I hear my uncle saying to his son behind us. "I need some air, I can't breathe, it's so stifling in here!"

Surely it's father who's the one hogging all the good air for himself, and preventing everyone else from breathing; and yet just before he died he was so small, so thin, that he must have needed very little air.

In any case, anything is possible in the best of all possible worlds.

A stick of chewing gum suddenly appears in front of my eyes—my uncle is giving it to me with a knowing look in his eyes:

"It prevents your ears from popping."

"But we're not in a plane!"

He looks surprised and adds:

"It's the same thing, it's the same thing, listen to me, you have to be brave, don't worry, you're a man now, think about your mother, think about your future, it'll be hard at first, but things will work out... And of course we're here after all, you can count on me, and your lovely mother can also..."

"What a bastard!" my father whispers to me.

We're almost there. We must have been riding for quite a while; no one is talking, they're either tired or have nothing to say to each other anymore.

We reach the cemetery at last, everybody gets out. Handkerchiefs reappear. There is an unbelievable crowd of unbelievable people. I didn't know my father had so many friends…he spent most of his time alone, and lost in his thoughts, as if he were trying to find a truth that escaped him.

They made us stand in line, one behind the other, with our handkerchiefs in hand, while the casket passes in front of us, in the midst of flowers. People shake hands, kiss each other; a few women look like they might pass out because of the pain; they speak in loud voices and argue; they wonder how they will get back into town since the hearse drives to Père Lachaise cemetery but doesn't drive back downtown.

It's done, the casket is on the ground, a man all in black and all in beard, the undertaker, chants in Hebrew and calls the rabbi who is on duty and who was waiting discreetly and almost fearfully to be called upon.

The rabbi is a lost soul who wanders around the cemetery from one plot to the next, desperately searching for a fee. He goes from burial to burial, from one tomb to the other just like an unemployed actor who is ready for anything while he haunts the television studios…

He's wearing a long black coat and an old hat, a hat in this heat! He looks like a Polish Jew who just escaped from a concentration camp…

All he needs is a suitcase to be on his way to Bergen–
Belsen... He says his prayers mechanically and very
quickly, I can't make out a word he's saying, nobody
else can understand what he's saying either... Every ten
phrases there's this little gesture he makes with his hand
and one of the crying people in attendance steps up, and
delicately places a ten franc note on the casket.

After a while there are so many bills on top of the
coffin that the rabbi signals that the prayer is over and
stuffs them quickly in his pockets; they start hugging
again and they cry their joy as they meet cousins they
hadn't seen in ten years and finally they leave as they
keep on chattering with one another. My mother returns
home with my uncle, they have all found a ride...

The party's over. The ceremony is finished, the
obligation has been fulfilled, my father is buried and I
stay there, disheveled, empty eyed, dumbfounded. ...

The rabbi comes over and shakes my hand... He
looks like the rabbi in Tunis who officiated at my Bar-
Mitzvah. I was ashamed, so ashamed. Here I am,
supposedly becoming a man and I'm small, so small, like
an ugly stunted child, and I am in a wheel chair, and I get
up to go to the Torah and I grab my crutches, and I trip
and fall like a wooden puppet.

My cousin sneers aloud and my older brother, my
older brother who is so good to me, comes over and
helps me up. I hate him for being so tall and I'm
ashamed.

Why are we all here anyway? Nobody really believes
in this synagogue where we're all disguised in our
Sabbath best. My father isn't even wearing a yarmulke

and has a handkerchief on his head instead and my grandfather is wearing a hat. I learned my prayers phonetically, pretending that I know Hebrew but I have no idea what I'm saying or what I'm supposed to be saying, or what I'm expected to feel. We become Jewish once a year, at home for Yom Kippur; we fast, go to the synagogue late in the afternoon, and come back home happy to be forgiven…but forgiven for what, I wonder?

But we feel that we are Jewish…

The extended family is more Jewish than we are; we're heathens who believe in nothing… Maybe they have reasons to be religious, while on our side of the family...

So why be here, in this synagogue, today? So that I can look ridiculous? So that I can be ashamed? To enjoy the circus of my becoming a man?

The rabbi smiles at me with a big smile that tries to be so kind and compassionate. He's wearing an old black coat and hat; he looks like a Polish Jew on his way to Bergen-Belsen.

Everything is mixed up, Tunis, Paris, the cemetery and the synagogue, the dead, and the living.

I am also alive, and what gives me the right to be alive?

The last car goes by and I can cross the street, and seven years after his death I'm still walking the streets of Paris thinking about my dead father. I've been walking without any help… for only twelve years and I'm twenty-seven. Do you know what it means after all these years to be able to look at someone straight in the eyes without having to lift one's head? I know…I've managed to defeat my illness, to overcome my fate. I am walking.

A month ago I started growing a mustache and they tell me that I look good with it, that it makes me look even wilder. Actually, I now look like what I hate the most, a wog. They say I have beautiful lips, so every morning I trim my mustache to show off my upper lip and use my mouth as a means of seduction… When people don't like me, when I can't make them like me, I feel like dying.

Actually I have a small but full mouth, the small full mouth of a licorice eater. Add a tiny round and willful chin and then I appear totally ridiculous! I look like a comic book character. But my nose saves me! It's long, hooked, and bent, and has a life of its own, a nose with character.

Rather small greenish eyes, with heavy eyelids that carefully trimmed eyebrows attempt to enlarge. But a look, a look that is amused, sad, ironic, desperate, impassioned, burning, yes, all that and more!

"He has his father's eyes!"

"I hope my father had beautiful eyes, madam."

"He was the most popular man in town!" she said as she giggled.

He looked like Rudolf Valentino, so handsome, so distinguished, with that look…that look. So my look must be devastating… A thoughtful crease between the eyes, a large strong forehead and curly black hair around my face… Real Frenchmen look at me with some misgivings, I don't look like them, I don't look like an Italian, and I don't look like an Arab.

France is unable to label me, I don't look like anybody, just a bit like a wog.

I really discovered what France was all about when I was given the grotesque privilege of attending the University of Paris, at Nanterre, to complete my advanced degree in my highly enriching literary studies... What a joke! One more slapstick comedy! One more bit of fraud... I spent three years wasting my time with shitty professors who yawned as they taught us French literature... Thankfully, the shanty town was nearby, at least we had some laughs with all those assholes who were dreaming of restructuring the world and were getting ready for May 1968.

Nanterre, the new university, a building in the middle of nowhere, that is actually in the middle of a shantytown inhabited by the most wretched children of French society. It looks like a Johannesburg slum. You get off the train and must walk along a makeshift pathway boarded by cardboard and metal shacks to go and hear the geniuses of French culture, and then people wonder why students march in the streets with banners, and burn cars, and throw Molotov cocktails.

Nanterre, the powder keg of the far left... The Senegalese Mamadou had quietly transformed the Nanterre dormitories into brothels... The female students would get paid for their services and he would grab all the money, like a pimp in Pigalle, all dressed up in a silk suit with a pink shirt and polka dot tie. But those girls were communists, or rather extreme "gauchistes," and by working as whores for Mamadou they were convinced that they were helping the poor in the third world who were being exploited for decades by their leaders. Actually Mamadou must have also had some unusual masculine attributes that the young ladies at the new university could verify very freely and with undeniable pleasure since all this was done in the name of the "gauchiste" cause.

Just as the majority of the professors of the great university, who were teaching tomorrow's leadership had only one idea on their mind, to fuck as many young silly chicks who surrendered for the greater glory of literature... I remember in particular Professor Robert Corbeau, a handsome sixty-year-old novelist who at the end of each master class in the great amphitheater makes a show of such incredible generosity and consideration when he announces on the microphone that he still has space in his car to drive just one person back to Paris. He never mentions that he drives a small sports car with only two seats, and as soon as the young lass sits next to him he immediately slips his hand up her thighs and makes obscene comments thinking that they would be exciting.

Nanterre, is where I made my debut as an actor and where I discovered that the theater is way of escaping reality, mostly because I love to act in the absurd plays of Ionesco. Nanterre, is the hotbed of modern rejection, and the symbol of the disintegration of a culture and the death of a civilization.

The dumb antics of Nanterre drive me astray, there's nothing to gain from rehashing the same old stories. When I walk around Paris, I always take the same itinerary, I must not like surprises. I wear the same jeans, the same black leather jacket, the same turtleneck sweater…

I dress like a thug because I don't have the money to be dressed like a lord and it kills me… but I'd love to wear silk shirts and linen suits, and I hate those who actually do wear linen suits. Actually I hate just about everybody! I hate men who are irresponsible, loose women, misbehaved children, abusive grand fathers, sniveling grandmothers, seductive uncles, love hungry aunts, stupid cousins, nosy neighbors, boring acquaintances, unfaithful friends, useless encounters and even those I don't get to meet, since they don't exist.

I almost hate everybody, I almost despise everybody.

"I don't want to be loved, I just want to be feared."

Either Caligula or Nero. Oh ! If only I could play Nero, I'd show them, or if not then Figaro, yes Figaro or Harlequin or Treplev, or Romeo, or Chekhov or Shakespeare. Shit! I'll show them what real talent is all about!

I have a kind of special affinity for the word shit. My mother couldn't stand hearing me say shit, she wanted me to have good manners.

I can hear her raspy voice:

"Julien, who taught you to use that word, don't say it!"

"Yes, mother."

"I will tell your father"

"Yes, mother"

"I know he lets you get away with everything, but this is too much, he's so weak with you it's awful, he

15

allows you anything, thank goodness I'm around, because otherwise you'd be totally spoiled."

"Yes, mother."

"What am I going to do with you..? You tell me... Can you tell me what we're to do with you? You won't always have everything and when we won't be around anymore what will you do, tell me? Answer me when I talk to you!"

"Yes, mother."

"I can't stand it, answer me or I'll slap you!"

"Shit! Mother."

In Paris, in the early hours, you mostly run into cleaning ladies on their way to work, they look so happy, and without any worries at all. I could be a cleaning lady! Yes, that's what I should have been! How do you say that about a man? A cleaning man, I guess? I would stay at home all day, empty the ashtrays still filled with the smoke of all that idle chatter, make beds filled with dreams, and above all with frustrations, and serve at the table, Mr. and Mrs.! I have no responsibilities...

"Julien! You know I like the roast very well done!

"Very well, madam!"

That's my kind of responsibility! My life will be about eating and drinking well, going for a walk on Sundays on the avenue de Wagram or the Place de la Muette, with the Spanish maid servants and perhaps manage to pick up one of them from time to time. Nice life that of a maid, or a flunky.

I'm going to consider it seriously...

Unless that is the kind of woman I truly want to meet...a sweet, understanding and tender cleaning lady, someone who makes no mistakes, and excuses those made by everyone else! People will say about her:

"It's great, she can get everything done, her work, her house, and her husband, who is not such an easy person to deal with on a daily basis, she's really the perfect woman."

One day, just like that, on some street corner, where else? I'll find the woman of my life, the one I met so often in my dreams. I often have this strange and wonderful dream of a woman I love, and who loves me, and as we look into each other's eyes we'll dance with castanets and cleated shoes, and we'll go far, very far away, to a country that resembles me, and we'll never leave each other. I still have childlike dreams, I'm a real loser! I can't look at myself in a mirror, or a window, or even catch my reflection in a puddle, without breaking out in hives, thinking about how horrible I look and how I wish I could disappear forever... I'm in a panic...a panic...

The panic that I can never shrug off is how they make me feel; the horror of being a Jew, a kike, a sheeny, a Juden, Juden Raus, death to the Jews, dirty Jew, fucking Jew...Jew or rug peddler. I can't tell, it's probably the same thing.... I don't know, I don't know anymore, I never knew... A poor Jew... A poor Jew. Come on! There is no such thing as a poor Jew as they all say, even the Mexicans say so.

I am proud to be a Jew but nobody wants to allow me that luxury.

JUDEN RAUS... We'll burn them, castrate them, decapitate them, gas them, chop them up, turn them into lampshades, hang them, rape them, humiliate them, those fucking rich Jews, and the poor Jews as well, they're all the same.

My father never talked to me about it, he never discussed it, never said anything, he kept quiet…Speak up! Say something! A conspiracy of silence…I keep quiet, you keep quiet, they keep quiet…He wouldn't talk about it, and it remained taboo despite my insistence, despite the usual questions repeated again and again.

Dad, please tell me how it was.

"What?"

"How was it inside that camp? Were you really there?"

"Yes, I was there."

"How was it?"

"I don't know anymore."

"What do you mean you don't know, tell me, I want to know, tell me."

"I forgot."

He's either lying, or he's fearful, or he wants to protect me because that's one thing you don't forget, I don't in any case, do I?

No, I don't forget, it's there always in my head, always there in my heart, in my belly, in my balls… So please stop saying so smugly…he's a Jew.

I happen to know many poor Jews, many stupid Jews, many Jews of little or no consequence…

The panic…the panic that came before…and the panic even now. Maybe to disappear is the solution. To…disappear… Then I return, as an invisible man to see if people are sad after I'm dead and I would say:

"Don't cry, I'm not dead, look, here I am…"

To be able to comfort, to have the ability to comfort someone, that's all I ask for.

I don't want to fail, I'm too frightened, a terrible fear, terrifying, obsessive, paralyzing. I don't want to die without having known what true beauty is, without having seen something big and powerful, or else I want to die immediately to have the excuse of having run out of time! I don't wish to live without creating something that will change the world! I feel so much untapped energy within myself! I could lift up the whole world! I don't want to feel the days drifting by, just melting away; my hair falling out; my skin having deeper wrinkles; my belly growing larger; my life seeping away; getting old! I don't want to get older without having done anything! I don't give a damn about wisdom, maturity and that whole menagerie.

I want things to happen, now.

I'm going to write a book and once it gets published I'll kill myself.

I shall write a book and if they don't publish it I'll kill myself… I'm going around in circles, ring around the rosy, but I have no lamb, little red riding hood, red like the kitchen, like the ants I burn to death, like the blood of the bulls, I can't wait to go to sleep tonight.

I hate sleeping by myself so I just pick up anyone along the way, a girl who is lost just like me, who also hates to sleep alone, and we spend the night together, alone even more alone, and the next morning we part, alone, even more alone once more, and awfully sad, sad enough to cry, and the assholes tell me that I'm a Casanova, what a joke! I, Casanova? A sad loser still looking for himself without ever finding out who he is and that's what is killing him! That's the truth!

I, Casanova? A noble master, and a mean individual?

Rather, an ugly little shit head! Yes, that's more like it! That's the truth!

And now here I am walking, walking in Paris twenty years later. I'm walking constantly to find my legs, to find the life that had been taken away from me a long time ago.

Tunis is so far and yet so close... You never really become someone else, just another part of yourself, the part that was denied and forgotten.

I'm fed up with walking and I feel like a cup of coffee! It will cost me 80 centimes... So what, I'll see, I'll walk home instead of taking the metro, it'll be good exercise. Exercise, my obsession, to always exercise all the time, all my life, at every turn, at every moment those fucking exercises, every day for fourteen years, nothing elsc...But why me? Why?

"Are you going to play soccer?"

"I can't, I'm exercising."

"Are you going to play tennis?"

"I can't, I'm exercising."

"Are you going to the movies?"

"I can't, I'm exercising."

"Are you going to the whorehouse?"

"I can't I'm exercising."

"Are you going to a surprise party?"

"I can't, I'm exercising."

"You...."

"I can't, I'm exercising."

"Are you coming to my house tomorrow?"

"I can't, I'm exercising."

"Are you coming to the country this Sunday?"

"I can't, I'm exercising."

"Do you want to play marbles?"

"No, I'm exercising."

"Do you..."

"No, I..."

"Do you..."

"No, I..."

"Do you..."

"No, I..."

I have fourteen years to catch up! Do you know how long that is, fourteen years, you bunch of assholes, and losers. For fourteen years I would hear and repeat, panting four hours a day, one…two…three…four.

"So, today we're feeling a bit better, right my boy, you'll see we're going to get there. In three months, in four months you'll be doing much better."

Three months, four months?... It went on for fourteen years. You rotten doctor, with your kindly ways, you're a liar, but such a bad liar that it makes me heartsick.

"Okay, let's go. One, two, three, four."

It hurts, it hurts so much.

"Are you ok, my boy?"

"Yes, I'm feeling fine!"

"It doesn't hurt?"

"No, no, not at all."

It hurts, it hurts so much.

"Let's measure you now, okay my boy?"

"If you wish."

I really hate it when that man calls me 'my boy.' It hurts so much…my legs hurt, my heart hurts and my soul hurts too. Why me? Why? What did I do to deserve all this…

"In life you get what you deserve."

"You reap what you sow."

And you Dad, did you get what you deserved? The camp, a son who dies at age 26, another son, me, who is a cripple, an ugly invalid, and finally you, dying like a penniless bum in a hospital bed in Asnières at age 59…

What did you do for fifty nine years? You idiot.

"All right, so let's take your measurements…

Well now… That's very good, you have increased by half a centimeter around the thigh in four months, that's great."

"Great?"

"Why sure, that's good, very good, you'll see, we'll get there."

Half a centimeter in four months, at this rate it'll take me twenty years to make it and he thinks it's great. If I could I'd punch this doctor, I may be a cripple and a truly pathetic sight but I'm not stupid.

"You know something doctor, you're nothing but an asshole!"

He left without saying a word and I could hear him repeating everything to my mother, not only did I have a lousy disposition but I also hadn't the slightest chance of recovering, the slightest chance of walking, or the slightest chance of leading a normal life.

Not a chance? But you don't know who I am, you shitty doctor, you'll see, I'm going to make it. Let's go

Julien "my boy," go at it again on your own, once "the scientist" leaves every morning after four hours of exercises you keep on going by yourself, you take yourself to the limit, the minute you're alone. You know the exercises by heart after all this time, so go for it again and again and again instead of burning the ants to death and wasting your time.

"One, two, three, four."

Oh, god, it hurts. I want to do more!

"One, two, three, four."

I can't take it. One more time.

"One, two, three, four."

I'm sweating, I'm all wet, drenched to the bone and they'll keep on repeating that I tried to jerk off once again.

"One, two, three, four. One, two, three, four."

"Dad, do you think I'll be able to walk someday?"

"One, two, three, four."

"That I'll be able to run, dance, dance in the sky like Peter Pan?"

"One, two, three, four, more, more."

"He won't be able to lead a normal life."

"One, two, three, four."

"But he will, you'll see."

"One, two, three, four."

All day I will do my exercises and I'll get there through sheer willpower just to prove to them that they are wrong. They'll all die of spite but I will walk, I'll dance and one day I'll get married and I'll have a son who won't be like me, he'll be big and strong, an athlete, a champion, and he'll run the marathon.

"1, 2, 3, 4"

"I'll try…"

"1, 2, 3, 4"

To find a woman…

"1,2, 3, 4"

Who'll love me…

"1, 2, 3, 4"

Whom I'll also love…

"1, 2, 3, 4"

Not like mom and Dad…

"1, 2, 3, 4"

Who cheat on each other and don't play by the rules…

"1, 2, 3, 4"

Who hate each other…

"1, 2, 3, 4"

As much as I hate them.

Okay, I'll go have that cup of coffee and spend the 80 cents. I enter the café. There should always be someone waiting for me! I have an appointment? With whom? Oh, I'll end up finding someone to have an appointment with, I have until this evening, to find, invent or dream someone up. How strange, I don't see anyone I know inside… All the well-bred Frenchmen, even the lowliest down-trodden slobs, look at me as though I had just arrived from another planet…

But why do they look at me like that, what's so different about me? I'd like to meet someone so badly, someone who knows me, but nobody knows me in this fucking town except for other actors who are just as lonely as I am. No one knows me. Where am I? Who wants me? I'm in Paris alone, walking around in search of friendship, of something…and then nothing, no one, but why me? I'll still go and have a cup of coffee at the counter and pretend to be waiting for someone who will not show up so that the people around me will not think I am alone.

Even in the street I don't want to look like I'm alone, it's too sad. When I walk, I always walk very fast with a specific goal in mind even though I don't even know what it is. I don't want people to think I'm just taking a stroll or they may think I'm a male prostitute. When I do let myself go and actually take a stroll, I feel all those eyes looking at me filled with doubts, often with hatred, sometimes with desire, heavy looks that intrude upon me, of men and women, old and young! Reptilian looks that leave their traces of foamy spittle on my cheeks.

Go away! Leave me alone! I don't want to get to know you…. I only want people that smile as they look at me without any second thoughts. Several times I've even been groped in the metro by the professionals who hang around in the crowds, those who rub themselves up against you, the guys who lurk behind the urinals, who give each other a slimy look, quickly, shamefully and sniff one another in their excitement like dogs in heat.

What filth.

"Julien, you must be careful, you know there are some men who are real pigs."

"Yes, mother."

"Never follow anybody! Never listen to anyone! Don't trust anybody. Especially in your condition. Even if they offer you candy."

"Yes, mother"

In my condition? Does she also think I'm retarded?

Just to disobey her and get on her nerves I would be ready to go if a pig has something to offer; He will give me candy, and he'll take me to the movies, maybe he'll hold my hand and say nice things to me, it'll feel different, for a change.

I lean on the counter in the café.

"A cup of coffee, please."

I say it casually, in a relaxed and almost tired way, just to show some bearing, bearing, ...bearing, at any price, always create the impression that you've just done or are about to do something important. The waiter either didn't hear me, or pretends he didn't... Yes I'm convinced that he's doing it on purpose. I'll have to start over and order my coffee a second time. What if I just walked out as if I couldn't bear waiting! And then go where? After all, having a cup of coffee will waste all of five, maybe even ten minutes. I can just hear them repeating incessantly, drumming it into me:

"He'd be better off getting a job; he wouldn't have time to be bored. He'll regret it later on when he's a failure. An actor! He wants to be an actor, that's really off the wall. Why not become a singer while he's at it? An opera singer, what a joke! He'll regret it later on, life goes by very quickly. The world belongs to those who get up early. You have to be bold, you get out of it whatever you put into it, the early bird catches the worm, and blah...blah... blah...

Work, and do what? Huh? What? What?

Money. Money... You have to make money, more money always more... I don't want a little nine to-five job, I couldn't take an inconsequential position. I'd rather die, just like a big wine skin draining itself out.

To croak, be buried, rot, make worms, and all that, all that suffering for nothing, nothing. To die for nothing, to live for nothing, to die in order to live, to live in order to die, without having done anything, seen anything, to go through those exercises in order to die! To die without having had every woman in the world, without having had everything there is to eat, to drink, everything! Death? Death? Death!

What is death? To go to sleep one day and wake up dead, is that it? If that's what it is then it's very tempting! To wake up and say: fine, now I'm dead. I'm finally at peace, I'm free at last, I am dead. I could then tell everybody, you know now I don't give damn about anything because I'm dead. You can hurt me, ignore me, hate me, humiliate me; I don't give a hoot because I'm dead. I'll run through the streets yelling "Fuck you, I'm dead, I'm dead!"

Isn't that great?

I can go anywhere without anyone seeing me, enter apartments, penetrate other people's brains, their hearts, and find out what they're thinking.

I'll finally find out why people are so mean.

"Man is born good." What a pathetic sod that guy Rousseau must have been. To find out why people are cruel, selfish, pitiless, loveless, to know why people are all losers, why they are mentally impotent, to discover why man has remained at that stage of underdevelopment... Now that's a real mission, something truly useful, that's going to be my coming career.

"May I take your order sir?... Sir?"

I pretend I can't hear him, my turn to be a shit. He insists.

"What'll it be sir?"

"Oh, sorry, I was thinking of something else... Coffee."

I should have pretended that I was tired instead, that I was being tormented by a difficult problem or that I had just pulled off a tough caper. I passed up a good opportunity to play a role, something I need so badly, I'll show them, I'll prove it to them, I'll force them to admit that I have talent, a lot of talent, an immense talent, that I am a great actor... who hasn't had the opportunity to prove himself... In any case they couldn't care less about my talent, what they want is a name the public can recognize that would fill the theaters, sell tickets, a star! Ah, yes! A name, what crap, what a fraud.

What about the art of acting?

I can offer a lot, I know, I feel it, I have so many things to say... I can play any role, be it dramatic or comic, I can make you laugh, cry, I can do anything

Tania, my drama teacher told me as much... The first time I played a scene in her class...

She said: "Are you a Jew or a Slav? Only Jews and Slavs have that kind of 'soul' ... You can come to my class..."

I answered, "But Mrs. Balachova unfortunately I'm unable to pay for the classes..."

She looked at me very much annoyed...

"But no one is asking you to pay anything," she answered. "And call me Tania. I'm taking you in my class…"

Since then I've been an actor in search of a part…

But they need a name… Ah! A name! In the name of the Father, of the Son and of the Holy Ghost, amen!

It's hard being an actor in France when you're the son of a small-time Jew from North Africa, the son of a nobody. I suddenly have an idea of genius, I'll change my name. Then glory will be all mine. Glory. I'll be triumphant.

I am a great Roman general after five years of conquest and victories returned to Rome cheered on by thousands of people. Women fell to his feet, begging him for a glance and me, magnificent and disdainful on my chariot drawn by five white stallions. Was it five or six?

"That'll be 90 centimes sir…"

"The tip is not included… Sir…"

He interrupts my dreams of glory again with his small-time requests.

I must leave this café, everybody is smoking and you can barely breathe. It's filled with little chicks who are so irritating when they make faces while trying to be cute. They cough and smoke at the same time while they drink Coca Cola… It's full of crummy students who act as though they're going to run the country some day, and provincials who are thrilled to be living in Paris. Everyone is talking at the same time like a bunch of Italians and the noise is deafening, bone crushing and deadly.

Back in the street, the sky is covered with dark grey clouds and Paris stinks of dog shit.

The street hasn't changed, it's the same as yesterday, and tomorrow, no, not tomorrow because by then I will have blown everything up, it can't go on like this, there is a malaise... It is inconceivable that someone like me should be completely ignored. Something doesn't work. I have no name, nobody knows me, I don't know anybody, fine... But... That must change, I'll get back at all those bastards! I hate them. I feel like throwing up on them, I feel red blotches coming over my face, coffee always does this to me.

"Can't you look where you're going?"

Had I been wearing a silk suit that clown wouldn't have talked to me like that. Ah! Catherine, if I had a silk suit you wouldn't have left me!

I hate you because you see me at a low point and I can't stand it. I'd rather be dead to you, I'd rather set fire to myself, waste away. I feel like dying of shame, of rage, of disgust. Not like that asshole, Mike, who drives me in his red Ford Mustang, the red car of a jerk, he must think he's a fireman or something. I met him at the drama classes, he wants to be an actor, he's the son of a famous movie actress, he's tall, blond with blue eyes, and plays at being an American.

He is a very bad actor but he is somebody's son. He also inherited mountains of cash, soon he'll probably be the lead in a worthless vaudeville show. He's happy, so happy he makes me sick and gives me a stomach ache just thinking about it.

How can such an animal be so happy?

To top things off he even says he's happy.

Catherine you should have waited, waited for me, understood, understood me, after it will be too late. I must tell
this to someone but to whom? To whom? Who can hear
me, who....

I feel like looking at myself, seeing myself to feel
sorry about myself, how sad I am, and how lonely, tears
roll down my cheeks!

I'm fed up! So fed up! What am I going to do about
my own fucking life, my own very fucked-up life. This
can go on ten days, ten months or ten years.

I've got to make a phone call, I must...

"I'd like a token for the phone please."

"Yes, just a second, can't you see I'm busy?"

"Yes, ma'am."

"Sixty centimes."

"Excuse me?"

"Sixty centimes! Are you deaf or what?"

"Oh, I beg your pardon, madam!"

"Yeah, sure, I know all about your kind of people."

"Stupid bitch!"

I didn't dare say that to her face but mumbled it to
myself on my way to the phone booth.

"Hello, Jean? It's Julien... How are you?"

"Fine, thanks, and you?"

"Very good, I've got a lot of things going."

"Great, I'm happy for you!"

"Any news, otherwise?"

"The same old stuff, the ships sinks, the rats jump
overboard and try to stay afloat. Last night I met
Philippe, he's in bad, bad shit, the blackest shit possible.
You know *The Great Game* is a colossal fiasco, he lost

his shirt with that movie, and he's in debt up to his neck."

The Great Game being a failure is really no surprise, an absurd movie about nothing where Philippe thought of himself at the same time as the reincarnation of Truffaut and of André Breton, his beloved Pope of Surrealism. Philippe wanted to produce the movie he had written, he put all his chips on the table and assembled all his buddies and a few stars who had lost their stardom years ago... He picked Pascale Baudret for the female role only because he is secretly fucking her since she's married to a very rich doctor who I suspect has financed the whole adventure without even realizing it; her brother, the popular singer Hughes Dufray will write the musical score and will bleat out something...Philippe had offered me a part commensurate with my talent: that of a young man who thinks he's the double of the ghost of his best friend, in this case played by Jean. This art movie will be shot on location in a big country house and we spend three weeks squeezing our brains trying to make some sense out of this monument of intellectual pretentiousness that Philippe calls his public declaration on what the new cinema should really be. Actually he spends more of his time in Pascale's bedroom than on the set...but we are all being collectively creative and share in friendship and pleasure a vast number of bottles of red wine and Philippe furthermore has found a way to pay us enough money so that we can survive for the next three months. We are happy, we're in the movies, we are actors and even better than that, we are artists.

We return to Paris, we are all convinced that this is at last our ticket into the world of filmmaking, we'll be celebrated as the new creative generation and our future is now guaranteed.

Philippe who thinks of everything and doesn't leave a single stone unturned has asked Sophie Tatischeff to edit the film. Sophie is the daughter of the famous Jacques Tati, the maker of well-known films like *Mr. Hulot's Vacation* and *Traffic*. So the big day finally arrives, Philippe who is either sensitive to the proper decorum or just a megalomaniac has rented a projection room on the Champs-Elysées to show the edited version of the movie. He invited the great Jacques Tati himself who appears in his long coat, rust-colored scarf and his beat up little hat looking just like a caricature of himself.

He sits in the middle of the room and is rather silent, in all probability he must be concentrating. We all sit at some distance from him out of reverence and respect and while the movie is being shown we are on edge watching for every one of his reactions. But he doesn't show any kind of reaction and I conclude that he must be concentrating very hard. The lights are turned back on in the projection room, Philippe gets up and walks over to the great master solicitously …our eyes turn anxiously toward Monsieur Tati who raises his entire six foot three frame and says: "Philippe, you think too much…" and he leaves without adding anything else. We all are back on the Champs Elysées in total silence and each one goes home; I take the metro in a state of shock.

"Julien are you listening?"

"Yes, yes, Jean I'm here."

"I think Philippe is thinking about another movie, a very interesting topic, it's the story of a guy who suddenly one day realizes that the woman with whom he's been living and who has just left him is really...
The words become confused, I stop listening, Jean's voice gets lost in the telephone...

Where are you now, Catherine? Maybe you're laughing with him, eating with him or drinking with him.

Maybe you're interested in what he says and fall for his false charm and display of intelligence?

He's telling you that he's unhappy and you pretend to believe him, that you feel sympathy for him, he takes your hand and looks deep into your eyes with all that longing, he's got that seductive side smile, he's sure of himself, and you are taken by him, blush and then laugh! He tells you the same things I said to you the first time and you listen to him as though you were discovering something.

He says:

"It's odd I have a feeling I've always known you."

"Oh, really?"

"Yes, we are really connecting in a way I didn't think was possible anymore. You see...may I call you Catherine?"

"Yes of course!"

He's going much too fast, a bit of self respect please!

"You know Catherine, life is really strange and at the same time it's so fascinating!"

The asshole really has no imagination at all!

"What do you mean?"

Don't go down that slope, you know very well that to have that kind of conversation with a man is already like surrendering or at least giving him that impression.

"Well because...because..."

The poor bastard isn't doing too well.

"...because it always happens when you don't expect it."

"Yes...What do you really mean?"

Really, you disappoint me! This guy is frightening commonplace. All that, the pseudo intelligent sentimental crap, what people call the opening shots, you know that! What a joke, how sad, and how absurd life is! With everybody repeating the same stuff!

But no, not you, do something. This is too demeaning, not you, I loved you, we were both in the same Chekhov and Molière plays, I loved you, I see you and imagine you in such a completely different light, not like this, please, you must react! Just get up and leave without saying a word, without speaking, without turning around, with a smile like the Queen of England.

But I see you carrying on:

"I asked you... Bertrand, I asked you: what do you mean?"

"Well.. I actually... I can't really express it...instant understanding, the fact that we immediately and suddenly can communicate..."

Catherine, Catherine! Hogwash, blah, blah, blah!

Can't you see that he doesn't believe a word he's saying, that the only thing he wants is to get you in bed, and that's all. If you feel like it say so, and just stop the whole stinking charade.

Why are you using the same words with him as you did with me, with such little difficulty and with no remorse?

The words you said to me belong to us, they don't belong to everyone, I believed them, you believed them, we built castles in Spain together, we rebuilt the world, we saw each other on the world stage as Othello and Desdemona, we traveled through Italy together… Do you remember ?

You're too smart, too sensitive, too generous to listen to this kind of nonsense; you have too much talent to waste it with someone other than me.

Jealousy, I get so jealous I could die, a look, a gesture, an idea, an image makes me sick. I'm jealous of the present, of the past and the future, I'm even jealous of myself.

"Julien, you know the first time I saw you I wanted to sleep with you!"

"When you saw me walk? That really does sound ironic!"

"Why do you say that?"

"For no reason. You wouldn't understand anyway. So you see a guy walking and you feel like sleeping with him, that makes you a rotten little slut."

"But darling, it's you!"

"It's me! It's me! First of all nothing proves that I'm the same person now as the one you saw then? And it was only a reflection of who I am!

Anyway, I can't stand the thought that you desire someone, even if it's me!"

Catherine, I can't believe that you have already forgotten all the love I gave you... I probably don't represent much of anything to you anymore. You'll probably start collecting mementos of your past loves like all the others?

They keep them...they look at them and reassure themselves.

"To my dearest Madeleine, in memory of our summer of '71." They collect letters, yellowing pieces of paper, faded pissy looking photographs and they sigh.

"Yes, someone loved me!" they say as they look at those relics of their past loves.

"At least I've experienced love!"

"It's better than being alone!"

"I love him."

"I don't love him."

"I don't love him anymore."

"I love him, do I love him or don't I?"

And time goes by.

"I thought I loved him, but it wasn't true."

"I forced myself to love him to convince myself that I could be in love."

"And you know, I obviously had my own physical needs."

"It's not pleasant to always be alone."

"It's because of my parents!"

But everyone can be loved, me included. My brother told me once: "Don't worry, everybody can be loved, even you with the legs you have, will be."

I forgive him, he was cruel as you can be at age fifteen...

So Catherine if you do love this guy don't tell him about me at all, don't talk about me. Burn my letters, break the records I gave you, tear up the address books, change the furniture in our apartment, sell your clothes, change your hairdo, speak a different language, forget everything I taught you, be new, new, avoid the memories that have nothing to do with him otherwise you'll lose him just like you lost me... I don't exist, I no longer exist, I never existed ... Capish?

Maybe by now he's stroking your face and you love it and he goes on getting you drunk on his chatter and his empty smiles! No! Enough! Enough!

Enough!

I'm screaming "Enough!" into the phone and my poor friend Jean thinks I'm mad at him.

"I understand your saying 'enough'! The situation is unacceptable; no one knows what they should do anymore...I'm in such bad shit, how do I get out of it? ...Tell me...how do I fix it? Huh?"

"Fix what?"

"I don't know, fix nothing."

"See that Jean, we automatically recite those dialogs from Philippe's movie script, we're so mediocre that it's frightening, Jean. I'm not feeling good at all, I'm down in the dumps, I'm fed up, I can't take it, I feel like shooting myself."

"Don't talk nonsense! You've got prospects, you'll make it, and you're young. But in my case, it's all over...."

"Yes I have an incredible project. If it works I am saved, I'm finally out of the shit for good, fuck! I hope it works, but this time I'm really hopeful."

"I wish you well, Julien."

"Obviously if this goes through you'll work with me, you know we could ... I don't know... I need your help."

"Have you heard from Philippe at all?"

"No, nothing! Not a word. But, Jean, listen, you have to excuse me but I have to go, I have an appointment. Good bye for now, good bye Jean, we'll call each other again and get together."

"See you soon, good bye Julien, thanks for calling"

Click, click!

Jean, Jean my friend, my only real friend, honesty personified...What's going to happen to you in a world that doesn't fit you? You love the theater for the potential truth it offers but no one believes in your kind of theater. I can picture you with your gaunt face, your lanky body, your constant sense of humor... Jean, Jean what's going to happen to you? I don't want you to get lost too...

I never really had any friends.

Already as a teenager in Tunis I would invent friends with whom I'd go out on Saturday afternoons and rarely in the evenings. Nobody really wanted to spend much time with me, I was hard to take, I thought I knew everything, I had an opinion on every subject, and on top of all that I slowed everybody down so I'd end up in a neighborhood movie theater with John Wayne or Victor Mature and my favorite—Christopher Lee, Count Dracula...

They all quickly become my best friends… I love the movies, the actors and actresses; later on I'll be an actor and I'll go to Hollywood and become rich and famous. I buy all the movie magazines; I cut out the pictures of the stars and paste them in a little scrapbook. I make some funny and surprising montages: Marilyn Monroe becomes a victim of Peter Cushing, the terrible Doctor Frankenstein. Jayne Mansfield is tortured by Spencer Tracy as Mr. Hyde… I dream of becoming a director, a film writer, of making movies and managing a studio. I read about their lives, and their adventures, how they would get ready to play a part. I become Errol Flynn as Robin Hood, Charlton Heston as Ben Hur. I look at myself in the mirror and make faces in an attempt to look like them. Sometimes, often actually, I'd linger on the cleavage of Marilyn, Gina Lollobrigida, or Lana Turner. Then I'd look at myself in the mirror, throw the scrapbook on the floor and burst into tears.

My mother would bring me back to reality.

"Don't come back too late tonight."

"Yes, mom"

"As a rule in your condition you shouldn't be going out at night."

"Yes, mom."

"You know that your father and I have done everything we could so you could walk again, so…don't do anything dangerous."

"Yes, mom."

"And be careful to avoid meeting any bad people, in your condition."

"Yes, mom."

"Don't forget that you've been very sick."

"Sick? You call this being sick? Like a bad cold?"

"What are you saying? Are you listening to me?"

"Yes, mom."

"Don't forget your cane."

"Shit, mom!"

"I'll tell your father."

"Yes, mom."

My father...that failure with his tender-looking eyes...

I wish you had stayed alive just so you could see me succeed. How happy you would have been to see me on the stage, you'd have stopped everyone in the street to say, that's my son! He's in the theater, he's on the stage, he's a good actor my boy, he's my son, yes, bravo, my son.

My father... I haven't a single bad memory of you, and who can really brag of having no bad memories about his father? You tell me, you tell me who?

Me, me, I can, yes I can... Again I must set myself apart... I am narcissus, Narcisso Yepes, the herpes of Narcissus or a flower, a faded flower unable to bloom.

Daddy, I can't think of you without feeling like ripping my balls out! And one of these days I will cut my balls off and eat them! Viva la muerte! I'm a castrated bull without horns.

I am eight years old. I go up to his bed, on Sunday mornings while mom pretends she's reading.

"Dad let's go and wrestle on the bed, ok?"

"No, not now!"

I move closer to the bed anyway with my duck-like walk. I let my crutches fall on the floor. I jump, no, rather I trip onto the bed and pull myself painfully up to my father's level. It hurts but I like to wrestle. It hurts and I'm eight years old.

"Dad, Dad, look I'm the strongest! I'm holding you by the throat, by the legs, by your back, so you can't move anymore. How's that? Say that I'm the strongest, say it! But say it!"

"It's true, you're really a very tough guy! What strength! You beat me; you're like Tarzan, like Zorro…"

"Dad, Dad do you think I'll walk someday? That I'll really be strong? That I'll be able to run, to play soccer and dance!

Ah, to dance in the sky just like Peter Pan!"

Daddy, Daddy! Help me! Answer me! You have to help me, you're my father! You have to do everything for me and you can do nothing, I hate you. It's your fault if I'm likc this, you shouldn't have had me, when you came back from the camp you only weighed ninety pounds. It's your fault, you were too sick to give birth to me, since when do skeletons have children, since when do the dead create life, I hate you Dad, I hate you, you're not my hero! I hate you… I hate you.

Don't cry Daddy…don't cry… You'll see we'll go to the movies together and we'll eat some caramels and I won't leave you all alone in the afternoon, I swear and I'll buy you pistachios and we'll take walks together. You'll see Daddy you won't be ever be alone again, even if mother leaves you. Don't cry Daddy, you're my only friend, I swear it's true. You know, when I'll get bigger and will be able to walk, I'll do so many great things for you. I'll be an actor and I'll put on scenes for you and you'll be proud of me and we'll go everywhere together, I promise you that, Dad.

He died before, that asshole!

I hate you Dad. I beg you, help me! I hate you.

"Julien help me die, help me!"

"Daddy I'm here with you."

"Yes but help, help me."

"How Daddy, tell me how?"

"Help me, help me."

"But I'm here, right here, next to you."

"Help me, help me."

"Yes, Daddy, yes."

"Help me, help me."

"Yes, Dad."

"Help me, help me."

"But, Dad…"

"Help, me."

"Daddy…"

"Help me, help me."

"Daaaaaad….!"

You were my only friend and now I have no more.

It's raining buckets now! Raining buckets! What a great cliché of a sentence! It was raining buckets, the blows came down hard, tough, harsh, crushing, see! Those wonderful adjectives language has to offer… "Allons enfants de la patrie…" "Let's go children of our homeland…the day of glory has come." No, it never came… He will never come… The Messiah, the golden age, friendship among men, it's all a pile of rubbish, of bullshit...

"I don't give a damn about God, the Devil and the holy altar." In any case screw you, I'm not Italian, I'm not Tunisian or Vietnamese and even less Palestinian, I'm nothing and I don't give a shit... no I do care, do I or don't I care?

Who I am and what I am?

I have to make a phone call...who do I call? Jean? No I just did that.

Then who else? Call myself, yeah, that's what I'll do, I'll call myself. Maybe I'll be at home, I'll ask how I'm doing, if I have any prospects, if I have a new girlfriend and all that stuff. Finally I'll make an appointment with myself and go for a walk with my own shadow that looks like my twin brother.

My shadow, the shadow of a shadow, the shadow of someone who will be, or rather, of someone who doesn't even exist.

Why is she looking at me like that? Yes, that one over there!

She craves me, I can sense it! The window we're both looking at is filled with grotesquely modern trinkets. Modernly grotesque! It's what they call the "designer" style. You grab some plastic, some steel, some glass, some leather, you mix everything and you become a great "design" stylist... A fraud, a joke! Anything is good enough to make money! Don't try to convince me that she's interested in this! If the answer is yes then it means she's an asshole! If it's no then it means she likes me.

She looks at me and smiles and I give her my hooded look, the Rudolf Valentino look my father used when he was the most popular guy in town before he was deported to the camp with the other Jews, before they drained the life out of him, before being crushed. I can sense her eyes are fluttering and she has a slight tremor in her body!

She looked at me with curiosity, then blushed, no she went pale… She's swaying a little. She must be some slut! And she's got an ass that'll give a corpse a fucking hard on! That slinky silk dress that wraps her body in a mold, that flirt! Damn it! She's so beautiful.

She: "Do you find modern style interesting?"

He: (Looks at her thinking: what a shithead!) "I really love the new shapes."

She: "I agree! There's something fascinating about it! Don't you think?"

He: (Man she really is a shit head!) "I would even go so far as saying that it's exciting."

She: "Yes, that's it, that's precisely it, the right word: exciting."

He: (Can't believe she's so dumb) "You must know that you have a really stunning ass. An ass that gives me a hard on, an ass that even eunuchs would go crazy about, MMMMMMMMMMMMM

She: "You bastard!"

He: "Actually you're even dumber than I imagined. Very well then, goodbye sweetheart."

She leaves, looking indignant… I'm sure she's going to turn around to look at me; she's really got a fantastic ass… There she is… I won… She turned around… I really am a genius.

Bastard! Bastard! We'll see about that…

Do women think I'm bastard? Perhaps. I really can't tell… I know that I like to look at them and make comments that are sometimes not well received at all; I shall try once again…

I'm going to sit on a park bench and watch the ladies walk by!

"Like a soldier who wants to die standing up." Poetry is totally useless, but useless things can be beautiful! Beautiful? "It's beautiful." Now that is a real statement. I heard it hundreds of times at the University of Nanterre… When you wanted to utter the final word on just about anything you'd say…"It's beautiful!" And everyone had a different opinion; an endless totally useless discussion would begin that lasted forever. The French know how to talk and say nothing just to make a show of their knowledge about everything that allows you to keep a conversation going all evening with the Attorney at Law Maurice Pommard and his two nieces, the Gauduchon sisters.

Miss Gauduchon and her sister are between twenty and twenty-five years old, clean, polished, homogenized, well bred, cultured, and unfucked, but very charming, with their unused vaginas, nubile and ready and willing to be married off!

They speak very intelligently, with lots of poise; they sit down in a distinguished manner on those crushed velour armchairs; they don't wear much makeup, just enough to enhance the natural beauty of their heritage, the Gauls perhaps or what's left of them.

"Official engagement of Miss Anne Gauduchon with the young and brilliant graduate of the École Polytechnique Albert Desballes. To both of them go our warmest and most sincere best wishes."

May god bless them and all that jazz! Amen!

Most conversations are meaningless and begin only to lecture using your own ideas better known as "opinions" and to attempt to show how intelligent you are with a wry little smile. The ideas and opinions are of no interest to anyone but from the beginning of the evening they are looking for an opening to inject the most brilliant statement and any device to achieve that purpose is good enough. Since all this has been repeated so many times everything is perfectly well rehearsed and people think they are sparkling, amusing, passionate and even seductive. I deeply feel for couples who have to listen to the same repetitious old stories, the usual predictable jokes, hundreds upon hundreds of times, enough to make you hate your partner or drive anyone crazy.

"What are the opportunities for a worker's son to reach important positions in our society compared with the child of a top company manager? Do they have the same opportunities?"

"Yes, of course."

"No, not at all."

"But yes, I tell you…"

"But it depends…"

"The real issue is very different…"

"Take me, for instance…"

I don't want to listen anymore, I don't want to hear. I sink in the deepest kind of boredom, but it goes on.

"What time is it?"

"Half past twelve."

"What strange weather we're having this season."

"And at this hour?"

"As you know here, in Paris, time is meaningless!"

"Well, there are no seasons left, as well!"

"Seasons are a figment of the imagination."

"Yes, that's correct, a figment."

"As you can see these days, sharp repartee is hard to come by!"

"There's no humor left, nobody has the time, everyone is running, racing...so, what kind of life is it anyway? It's exhausting."

"And all this because of the Americans, they really are fucking us up—you have to excuse my French—with their imperialism, their war, their conquests, Vietnam is a real disaster as an excuse to fight communism. Nobody really cares about any of that."

"You're right, and everybody is tired out anyway."

"If only that could be true!"

"Excuse me?"

"If only it were true!"

"What?"

"If only everyone could just croak, good evening madam."

"That guy is crazy."

If only everyone could just keel over... Then we'd have peace... I must say that I was lucky on that score ... Everybody around me dropped dead very quickly, they just vanished from view... Even though I never saw them, I knew they were there and I felt a bit stronger.

And...now perhaps very soon it'll be my mother's turn... During the afternoons around six I have to go to the hospital... She's been there for two months and I've been going there every day, well... almost every day... I am a good son; I bring her cigarettes and instant coffee and tell her everything is going well and that I have a lot of work. Not to reassure her or comfort her but because I can't bear her thinking that I'm a failure.

"I'm starting a movie next week."

"Oh! Really? That's wonderful, my son."

Tyrone Power, *The Eddie Duchin Story* I saw that movie with Dad fifteen years ago and I cried throughout the screening and my father held my hand all afternoon and we hugged when we walked out, it was so moving, so beautiful.

The emotion we felt could compete with the stories of the two orphans—Little Orphan Annie and Little Red Riding Hood.

Later on when I'll be a movie director I'll make a movie on the friendship between a father and a crippled son and everyone will cry and I'll have them hand out free tissues at the door just like they did for *Love Story* and I'll win the Oscar at the Academy Awards for the most incredibly schmaltzy movie of the year. That will be fantastic! Naturally in my movie my mother will be in the hospital and I'll limp along to pay her a visit every day.

I must admit that going to the hospital is no big chore, since I've got nothing to do, nothing, absolutely nothing to do. I also have an excuse to do nothing…I have to go to the hospital… So I have no time for anything else.

In any case I like going there; it's near the Gare de l'Est. And I must walk through the red-light district so that I can rehearse my next part in the movie where I may play the role of a pimp. I cross Pigalle, Anvers, Barbès, I look at the pictures of the porn movies, I try to roll my shoulders and look real tough when I walk to make them think I'm some kind of pimp making sure all his "girls" are working very hard!

I drag my feet somewhat, smoke one cigarette after the other, I'm here, and I'm alive! In short, I exist! I clench my jaws very tight, I try to look like a tough guy looking for trouble, and cut through the crowd with self-assurance.

"Hi honey, want to go out?"

No answer, never answer, just look a bit annoyed or condescending! But my eyes don't follow my thoughts and roam everywhere on the semi-naked bodies of those ladies. But I don't go beyond looking, I don't go upstairs as they say, with one of those ladies, I don't like whorehouses now and never did like them before.

"You want to come to the whorehouse?"

"No I'm doing my exercises!"

"We're all going to the whorehouse. We're all going to the whorehouse; we're all going to the whorehouse. Tough luck!"

"When I'm no longer sick I'll go and screw each and every one of them! I won't have to go to the whorehouse you bunch of assholes."

I did recover, I don't go to the whorehouse and I fuck them all, the ones I want; so I was right after all.

I hope I won't miss the next bus, which bus, where is it going? I don't know! We'll see. I'll wait at the bus stop in any case, with a worried look on my face, my hands in the pockets of my windbreaker. I'm wearing my stern look and my chin is jutting out willfully.

"Rarely have I seen such a willful child."

"He'll never make it."

"I'm not so sure, I think he'll be able to walk almost normally; you'll see."

"Maybe but he'll never succeed."

"With his kind of willpower he'll develop his legs and will be able to walk and go to faraway places."

"Yes but he'll never amount to anything."

"I don't agree with you, he'll walk."

"Yes, but never..."

I would have preferred to never walk and spend my whole life in a beautiful carriage with someone working for me saying "give me this, give me that, bring me this, bring me that." What a trip! As they say. To be able to ask for everything at all times because you're a cripple. "I'm hungry, I'm thirsty, I have to take a piss, I want to jerk off, I want to live."

All the pious souls in Tunis spoke of me in kindly Christian overtones. I can still hear them and they didn't even hide when they talked about me.

"They say he goes to school in his wheelchair and his driver carries him in his arms from the car to the wheelchair and then...to his pupil's desk inside the classroom."

"It's awful, he's so brave. In his place I'd have killed myself or… I don't know, I would have done…something."

"Yes he really deserves so much credit, never a complaint or even a sigh, always smiling."

"His parents are the ones you should feel sorry for; they understand, what a terrible life they must have…

"What does his father do?"

"He's really just a merchant, selling olives and olive oil, but he says he's an entrepreneur because it sounds better." They live in the wealthy neighborhood far away from the Jewish quarter and even farther from the Arab section. They behave as though they were French when they are actually Jews from here."

"You know those people are all the same! You don't really know where they come from, but they are everywhere and always obvious."

"Yes, but with a son who is only half alive they have so much to worry about."

"Oh! Yes, he doesn't really understand what's going on; he doesn't realize what he's putting everybody through, his family I mean, and his classmates."

"He's got to be a bit retarded otherwise it's inconceivable."

"Not at all, he's very smart, he's first in his class."

No, the nice French and very Christian lady is making a mistake, I was only the second not the first in my class. Many times I used to imagine that the first in the class would disappear or even die. In my mind I tried to ambush him so many times, I tried to strangle him twice, I shot him with guns, I tortured him to death, I blinded him, I poisoned him dozens of times and every morning there he was in the classroom, friendly to everyone, smiling like an idiot who is about to become a politician and who is a real son of a bitch. He could have gone into hiding and let a cripple move into first place, a crippled Jew instead of him that little shitty Frenchy with his flannel shirts and his handknitted sweaters. Besides, I'm three years younger than he is and…I am competing with him.

They say I am a genius. "He is so young! So ahead of every one else!" And very soon I will skip other classes and be with students who are five years older than I. They are all surprised that I am so young and yet in that class. They do not understand that all a cripple does is read, work, listen to music if he is privileged, if he is lucky, and has some money…

My parents had money, I feel bad for the cripples who are poor with few chances of making it. I feel sorry for them and yet at the same time I don't feel that I should be concerned after all; it's not my fault if they are crippled. They have to attempt to overcome their handicap as I did; it would be too easy to ask society to support you with the excuse that you didn't have the same opportunities to begin with.

I am the one the other kids look up to as their leader; they come up to me at recess; I remain sitting at my desk while they all go into the school yard to play, to run after one another and argue… I look at them from the classroom window and often one of them comes up to ask me for my advice about something or other, or how they should organize the next battle and I lay down the law like King Solomon sitting in my chair and they all listen to me, they fear me and laugh at me behind my back.

One day I tell them they all must, as they enter the classroom, kiss the side of the door as though there were a mezuzah... They all do it, even the non-Jews...The teacher who is another Frenchy doesn't understand and with his real French accent that we love so much says: "Gentlemen what does this circus mean?" ...I laugh so hard that he turns to me sternly and adds:

"Mr. Nessachar, I suppose I must thank you once again as the originator of this charade? Well then is that the case?"

So off I go into an explanation that in the Jewish religion, you must place a Mezuzah on the right side of every door except for the toilet and bathrooms. I add that the Mezuzah is the symbol of the Jewish faith: the love of a single God, the importance of study and the teaching of the Torah and the commitment to obey the laws of God. What I don't mention is that I don't really know any of this and that I had prepared for the "charade" the day before by doing some research. The teacher looks at me and says:

"Thank you for the lesson in the Jewish religion Mr. Nessachar. I'm sure we shall all benefit from it."

And him, the little Frenchy, the first in the class looks at me and is smiling as if to say:

"You can invent all you want it won't change anything: I'm still the first in the class." He also had the gall, the nerve, the obscene achievement of also being the first at gym! Well... shit! Spread some of it around! Be a little more generous, please!

Now, in Paris twenty years later I have my revenge…
It's my turn…I'm sure that the first in class, the little
Frenchy is today an excellent young company manager,
an executive director with a great future, that he must
have married Miss Beatrice Goduchon—the sister of
Anne and the niece of the famous attorney at law
Maurice Pommard.

He lives in the sixteenth arrondissement, and has one
child.

He works for his family from morning to night until
he's totally exhausted. As a boy my legs were dead while
now the first in the class has a limp prick every night and
Mrs. Young Manager's wife, née Beatrice Goduchon,
quenches her thirst two or three afternoons a week with
unemployed actors, with would be artists, exotic Jews, in
one word with guys more or less like me.

Maybe I even screwed the wife of the top student in
my class. I think about it, I am ecstatic and I smile. An
artist, the magic word that opens every door! Even the
one between the legs of the ladies Goduchon of this
world! And in the evening, relaxed, pleased and fulfilled
she talks about future projects with the Young Manager,
the managing director, who is convinced he has made her
happy and falls into a deep sleep thinking that fortunately
his wife is neither too sexual nor demanding.

He sleeps with a big angelic smile as he thinks of his
coming brood and wakes up the next morning still
smiling happily!

Sometimes life can be so beautiful!

When I think that sometimes I dream about that kind
of life: a stable job, an apartment, a wife.

For sure after some time I would certainly become an important man, a Young Manager, who also screws around once a week with a secretary, a sales girl, an artist while regretting that his own wife doesn't feel more sexy.

To dream the impossible dream!

People only really want whatever escapes their grasp, and they only love what they don't possess. If you live with the same person for too long boredom sets in. We still love each other, we respect and understand one another, we have tender gestures, we cuddle, but where did the passion go?

The passion is gone and you're bored to death. Actually after making love to the same person all the time, you don't know what to do, you forget how to make love, you look at one another gaga with love and you just fall asleep with quiet beatitude and a self-satisfied smile on your face.

Everyone seeks to be quickly reassured by carrying on a life useful to society, as a good citizen and a good mate that limiting relations with the same person all your life shall truly provide the greatest form of pleasure. One more lie eagerly repeated by our fathers and religious leaders.

For me having something new has always been the rule in my relationship with women and then even that became boring and I retreated to a monk's life, a masturbatory life, where pleasure is my only responsibility and comes only from me.

And yet André Breton's crazy love must really exist… to live only for one single person and to feel that that person also lives only for me.

To be brave enough to tell someone everything, everything you resent, everything you hold against her or him, everything you do not like, to endure hearing the same silly stories be repeated at various parties where he or she is attempting to impress the audience. To spend days waiting to see that person again, to breathe her in, finally to be able to live and not need anyone else, no more pride, no more prejudice, no more self esteem, no more secrets, but only exclusive love, crazy love, a dream come true to be double and in two places at once through someone else who becomes the center of the universe.

Something like that is too good to be true, you must leave it to those who dream about crazy love, that heart-breaker. I much prefer a new conquest that becomes disappointing too… Furthermore you can dazzle someone new, make her believe this…and that…while a woman you live with will immediately see through the device, everything is based on fraud and a disguise one uses or rather on the meaningless instant of sincerity that appears too rarely and doesn't mean anything anymore. Love is just a ludicrous sideshow.

"Excuse me sir, is this the right stop for bus number 92?"

"…"

"Excuse me but, sir, is this the right stop for bus number 92?"

"I couldn't care less about your bus stop, can't you understand that?"

"Please excuse me then, sir."

But why must she be so polite? Is she pulling my leg or what? "I must ask you to be so kind as to excuse me" she's really funny! I don't understand most women, they are so different from us! Léo Ferré said on television the other day, with his sunny southern French accent, "Women just screw you up, they only have uterine reactions" and he told how he ran after his wife with a hatchet to make her keep quiet. Their sense of humor is completely different from our own.

"Have you been waiting for the 92 for a long time?"

She's waking me up from my all important daydream with an absurd question

"Shit!" I answer imitating Léo Ferré's accent.

"Oh! You're really vulgar… I love it!"

"Bitch!" (Using the same accent).

"Oh, I can tell you're from the south, I can see it in your eyes!"

No, I'm from Tunis, you poor idiot, I'm a Tunisian Jew, I'm not from   Marseilles.

"Listen, why …don't you …just go fuck yourself!"

"Well here's my bus, are you taking it as well?"

"No!"

"Well then, see you soon perhaps, you are a charming man, so rough, almost brutal, Oh! You remind me of my brother, I just adore my brother, he's so different."

"My brother?"   Why are you talking about your brother?

Am I talking about my brother? Am I saying his name?

Fabien...Fabien... My brother ...

I never even knew you, or I didn't want to know you. I hated you because you were so tall, because you had blue eyes and a straight nose. You were six years older than I when you died, you were almost the same age I am now...How can you die at 26, how obscene. Six years older than I...you were hoping to get closer to me and I ignored you... I was jealous of you...

Fabien... I never understood a thing about you...while you admired my intelligence but you were ashamed of me...

Who wouldn't have been ashamed of such a human wreck, a stunted leftover of a child, with a ridiculous and battered body? You thought other people couldn't understand me or would laugh at me so you didn't want to show me to other people because you were so ashamed.

I wanted to be able to go out with you so much, to hold your hand, to look at you and be proud of you and proud to be with you and laugh, laugh out loud... You could have taught me how to say things girls love to hear, how to play billiards that you liked so much and tell me all about your Saturday nights at the "jazz club." Maybe even let me drive your sports car...

My brother, my brother, how I'd love to have someone I'd be able to call like that now, my brother, my brother...You see that even when I try to talk about you I'm actually talking about myself, I have such bad habits.

"He'll never make it."

"In my opinion, he'll be able to walk normally."

"Maybe, but… he'll never make it."

It's been six years since you died, Fabien…

…Six years…the telephone rings and startles me out of a deep sleep that night. … I was asleep, I who never sleep…

How could I be asleep on the night you were going to die? Have I no sense of my responsibilities?

"Hello, Galvani 9073, is this Mr. Julien Nessachar?"

"Yes."

"Your brother died in an automobile accident."

"Excuse me, what did you say?

"Your brother died in an automobile accident."

"What time is it?"

"Midnight."

It's midnight Dr. Schweitzer, midnight the "witching hour."

My brother has been murdered.

The phone becomes a huge terrifying object in my hand like a secret weapon that seems to swallow my fingers and my hand, I look at it dumbfounded…Wake up, but wake up?

"Hello, Mr. Nessachar, hello, hello…"

The poet is dead. Death in Venice. To Die in Madrid. Rendezvous with death… Six million dead…now its six million and one… one more!

"Hello, Mr. Nessachar? "

"Yes?"

"Are you all right?"

"I couldn't feel better, my brother is dead…everything's just fine."

"I'm sorry to have been so brutal."

"Don't worry about it…as you know we all have to die at one time or another, right?"

"Yes, of course. You are right. Monsieur Nessachar. Yes. And he didn't feel any pain!"

"Oh! Yes… well, that's even better, all is well that ends well. Good bye. Have a good evening."

"Yes, you know, whiplash…the "rabbit punch"…smack, his neck was broken in a single blow… Smack!"

"Smack?"

"Yes and on top of it the other occupants of the car actually don't even have a scratch…nothing…"

"Fantastic! What luck!"

"They have no injuries at all, his wife was spared, everyone else is fine, only him…Fate, bad luck, the wrong seat, the death seat."

"Only my brother, then? The death seat? The others are all right? Well that's lucky, a miracle."

"I'm really sorry, good night Mr. Nessachar."

Whiplash, the "rabbit punch" …but he hated the taste of rabbit…the rabbit's revenge… Smack… smack… Not even a scratch…Smack…

Now every time I eat rabbit I throw up on the carpet.

I never saw him again, I never saw his body alive or dead, I didn't go to his funeral nor anywhere else, he disappeared forever, he vanished, he doesn't exist, he's dead.

Period.

He is buried with the rest of the family, my father is dancing in the street, my mother became an old woman in two days, my brother's wife is free and I'm wondering who I am and where I am and whether life goes on even though he is dead. Life does go on for everybody even though my brother is dead.

A long, long time ago I used to have a brother and he died. My father said it was normal, that my brother was a rose and that god calls the most beautiful flowers in his garden to be near him…

A rose? Where does he find all that crap?

And then he added, "I hope he was wearing red socks, he looked so good in red," and he went into the street yelling: "Red socks, red socks! Red socks, red, red, red! God called him to his side."

God… God… Good…. Good

God… Goody Goody… God

Goody God… God Kong… King King…

Yes, I think I prefer King Kong to God…

Fabien, my brother you've been dead six years and it feels as if you never existed…I vaguely remember you like a friend I would play with during vacations, a friend I never had, and yet a long time ago there was someone somewhere who used to say, "My kid brother" in referring to me and I would say "My big brother." Referring to you. Somewhere, a long time ago.

Once for Christmas you gave me a fifty-franc note, it was in mother's kitchen. We both blushed and hugged self-consciously; I was thinking "What's going on with him? It's the first time he done anything for me." No that's not true, I was embarrassed because we hugged I had hated you so much as a kid, I always rejected every form of contact!

I must call his wife. After six years it's been like a conspiracy of silence: it is all happening as though he'd never even existed.

We never talk about it, I ask her no questions and she keeps silent! Is it out of modesty, or cowardice? I know nothing about him, nothing about them! Was he happy? Wasn't he? Who was he? Who? I have to ask her who he was, she must know. I need to know something, to find out more about my brother, my brother…

I'm going to write a book and once it gets published I'll commit suicide…

I thought that with time everything would be erased but on the contrary it exists more and more, time erases nothing. I don't want my brother to be dead, I don't want that, you hear! I don't want it…You are all dogs and I want my brother. I don't want to be reasonable, I don't want to forget, I don't want anything,

I want my brother.

If he could be here now we would be kings, but without him nothing is possible, nothing, nothing.

It's cold in Paris today, what strange weather for this season. The world is full of naughty boys.

No one ever discussed it again, nobody, nothing, not a word, not a sigh, not even a hint…just gone… And in fact not a single word from anybody about anybody at all. I never saw the family ever again, not a single one of them.

Not a word, not a sigh, nothing.

Jews do help each other you know!

Really? What a joke!

I never saw them again, the uncles, aunts, cousins etc.… The whole tribe, not one gesture, not one word, not a sigh… They all vanished forever in the Paris fog and left us, my mother and me without a penny in Paris… Wandering just as I am wandering right now, without knowing where to go. Yes, but Jews have a strong love of family… Yeah, yeah, sure… They did nothing at all…nothing…nothing…

They had their own problems, their lives, their anxieties… They were the forgotten ones of France's rout in North Africa

For the Tunisian Jews not a single penny not even a glance…

The official magnanimous French response was: the Jews, the Tunisian Jews are not even French, after all, they are not our problem. We have enough problems with the Algerian Jews who were clever enough to become French, so then we shouldn't be expected to take care of every kike in North Africa. Come on now! There are some limits to all this!

Nothing, nothing, not a sound, not a look, not a word, not a single gesture coming from anyone.

"He'll never make it."

"But he will, you'll see."

Shit, I'm dizzy, I'm going to throw up.

It's now almost one in the afternoon and I have been walking for a few hours heading nowhere.

"Are you feeling all right young man?"

"Leave me alone!"

"Come and have something in the café."

An older man elegantly dressed, with grey hair and blue eyes, tall and with a straight nose. He looks like a middle aged version of Fabien if he'd been given the time to get older.

"Come with me let me offer you something and you'll see you'll feel better."

"If you insist."

He slips a soft, well manicured hand under my arm as though I were some broad while he kept his glove on the other hand. The pressure of his hand on my arm is very delicate, much too delicate even, and somewhat slimy.

"Perhaps you're hungry? How about having lunch with me? I do have some time to kill, and it is lunchtime after all."

"If you wish."

So, I did it! I've crossed the Rubicon, and why not, after all?

In my condition…

This is the only missing touch to the picture of the young man lost in Paris, the unemployed actor ready for anything.

"Do you like a good steak? I know a restaurant around here where you can have the best steak in Paris."

Of course he would be the one to know all the top restaurants where you can order the "best" steak in Paris. People seem incapable of expressing any kind of clever thoughts. But he did sense that I liked meat, the cunning old man.

Those old fellows always have an incredible sixth sense about people. They've been walking the streets for so long in their search for "the best meat" and young blood to liven up their old skin they can spot an easy prey from afar.

"If you like."

"Yes and then you can tell me the whole story."

"What do you mean the whole story?"

"Everything."

"Why? Are you some kind of priest or something?"

"No! Not at all, I just said that to say something."

"If you are talking because you need to fill in the silence, don't say anything. It's much better... I'm not afraid of silence."

"You're not a very nice person, you know."

He's got the silly smile you'd expect from a playboy in Cannes on the Côte d'Azur hunting for company and youth.

"I've already been told as much!"

Fabien loved to go to Cannes every summer and liked to have people think he was a rich Spaniard on the make for starlets. He loved the movies but didn't understand a thing about them and kept on pestering me by asking stupid questions.

"Julien, have you seen Buñuel's last movie, what do you think of it?"

"Nothing."

"What do you mean nothing, do you think I should I go and see it?"

"Listen Fabien, just do what you want, ok."

"You're not very nice you know."

"I don't really care!"

I mix everything up, the old dirt bag, Fabien, me and everything else...

"What do you do for a living?"

"Who, me?"

"Yes, you!"

He really reminds me of Fabien it's uncanny.

"I don't do anything."

"What do you mean nothing?"

"Didn't you understand me, nothing, nothing at all! Should I draw you a picture?"

"But then how do you live?"

"What do you care, in any case I'm not living since I'm in the process of dying."

"Ah! Yes, I understand."

He smiles, that bastard.

"What do you understand?"

"No, nothing."

We cross the street and walk into the restaurant with the best steak in Paris, his shirt collar is open on his bull neck, his shirt is made of blue and white silk just like the one Fabien liked to wear.

"Fabien can I borrow your blue and white silk shirt?"

"What for?"

"To wear it!"

"It'll be too big for you! You'll float in it!"

Too big, too big, everyone knows you're six feet tall and that I am stunted child but I also know you're no good at school and that I'm first…no, second in my class. You're six years older than I and you're asking me to correct your homework. You're pathetic, my big brother.

I can memorize in ten minutes pieces of poetry that you repeat out loud for hours.

I took everything in my head while you put it in your legs.

"How old are you?"

"Twenty-seven and you?"

"How old do you think I am?"

"Fifty."

"Well, you're a bit harsh, I'm actually forty-three."

He's lying through his teeth, he's at least fifty, but he is in good shape, he must really take very good care of his skin with massages and an entire day in a spa.

…He looks somewhat ridiculous… But he also really does look like Fabien.

"You know that you are very handsome!"

"Yes I know! One is always handsome at twenty seven, don't you think?"

"I'm sure everyone likes your looks!"

"Yes, that's true, they do!"

"Do you like to be admired?"

"Yes, I do!"

He smells of lavender and Amsterdamer pipe tobacco, just like Fabien.

Maybe it is Fabien coming back to see what I have become and what I'm doing. He would be surprised and would admire me no doubt.

He'd see how I made it and he'd be happy and I'd be pleased to see him happy as well.

"What about you, what do you do?"

He smiles, he must be thinking that I'm really interested in his wallet.

He even smiles like my brother.

"Me?"

"Obviously, I'm referring to you, not to the guy crossing the street."

"You are very aggressive."

"Yes I know, I've often been told as much. Does it bother you?"

"I never said that I didn't like it, on the contrary, I like violent people who know what they want! Well here we are, this is the place."

Good, we are finally going to sit down and eat! Maybe with his mouth full he'll keep quiet for a few minutes.

The restaurant is pseudo upscale and stylishly chic, with a white tablecloth and the whole nine yards. The maitre d' looks very fashionable with a white towel on his arm like a hospital nurse. He leads us to the table with a wry smile, he's got the picture.

"Would you like to have a steak for two, it's more fun that way and it will put us in the right mood."

"What kind of mood?"

"Yes…it'll be more intimate? Don't you think?"
Really this guy will stop at nothing and he travels fast, he must be dying for it…for just about anything at all.

"You haven't answered me."

"Answered you about what?"

"As to what it is that you do?"

Again he gives me that self satisfied smile; he takes off his overcoat, the silk blue and white shirt is all mine now and I stare at it, he takes his time to answer me, clears his throat.

"I manage an import-export company. Yes, I know it doesn't sound that exotic or exciting but you know, you don't always get to choose. I actually wanted to be a surgeon but…

"You'll lend me your blue and white shirt one day."

He looks at me, surprised…. He looks at me and mumbles:

"I don't think it will fit you too well!"

There it is, all over again; when it's all over it starts up again… Seven years after his death Fabien still won't lend me his shirt.

"And why?"

"Because you're much more heavily built than I am!"

I burst out laughing; once again he gives me that dumb look of his.

"It doesn't matter, I'll try it I'm sure it'll fit me perfectly, yes, yes, perfectly."

"Well listen the easiest would be that I buy you one your size!"

"No, I prefer yours, that's the one I want! Do you hear me?"

"All right, don't get excited, I'll lend it to you, don't get angry I promise to let you try it!"

There! Fabien is finally going to loan me his shirt, maybe I'll even look like him! A blue and white silk shirt. I'll be very handsome! I'll look just like him! They'll say that I'm handsome! How elegant! What a classy guy! He looks so good in blue!

"Bordeaux or Beaujolais?"

"Excuse me?"

"The wine… Bordeaux or Beaujolais?"

"Bordeaux."

He orders a bottle and asks the sommelier a multitude of questions and details. He's wearing a pinky ring with a family crest on his left hand. An unbearably large crest with his initials that is simply too awful to look at. And he goes on talking; he talks about wines which he knows well since his family comes from the Bordeaux region and that ... I stop listening...

One day I thought I saw him, I thought it was Fabien's van that was at the red light on the rue de la Gaité, just behind the other car with the ridiculous advertising drawn on the sides: wear the Zou bra, pick the 3Z panties, keep your breasts well separated and you'll be ready for life. Ready for what? Why? I can't figure it out and they should be so courteous as to explain their offer better.

I hadn't seen him in three months at least, I ran behind the van, again and again, I yelled out:

"Fabien!... Fabien!..." the van was going faster and faster, at every stop,

At every red light, I thought I could catch up with it, and just when I was about to reach him, it was my bad luck that he'd take off once more even faster. He turned into the rue Delambre:

"Fabien!...Fabien!..."

He didn't hear me, he never did hear me...he never really listened to me, he doesn't have the time, he's working in the family business, he's off selling olives.

The old beau gives me a look filled with lust, and with his mouth full and the juices from the steak dripping from his puffy lips, he asks me:

"Isn't the steak simply delicious?"

"It's very good."

"So, tell me everything about you. What's your story?"

"And you?"

"Let's see, where should I begin? The tragedy of my life is that I wanted to be a surgeon. You see I…"

He's off again into his wild imaginings.

His words fall into the void of his stuffed mouth, and I lose the meaning of what he says.

I'm no longer listening to him and now he's just talking to himself, satisfied at the sound of his own voice.

Fabien was selling olives and I am selling hot air…in any case, running after his van was a waste of time even if he'd seen me, he wouldn't have really seen me. Who was that child with him? It couldn't have been his since he couldn't have children, my brother was sterile, his wife had a child three years after he died, the child he could never have, I will never forgive her… I hate the man who fathered that child, I should have been the one to have that child, me, the only person who could recreate my brother with our heritage, our heredity, our feelings… Was me! A child, my brother's child…It meant recreating him, to believe that he never had died, that he was here. Now I'm here and he's dead, I'll never forgive myself for being, for living…

"He'll never make it. Yes you'll see he will…"

"…Yes a surgeon, I'd have had the feeling of doing something useful. You know that people like me are terribly lonely and useless. To be a surgeon even for someone like me I don't know but… I could have…attempted…or whatever. I would have fought had I had a passion… I didn't want to be what I have become…but with me it becomes a real sickness. Already as a child I would leave my window open and dream that Peter Pan would come and join me in my bed."

Daddy, I'll dance, I'll dance in the sky just like Peter Pan, right?

"Peter Pan?"

"Yes Peter Pan, I hope you don't think that I'm being ridiculous!"

"No, not at all, not at all."

To walk, to dance like Peter Pan. Dad ?

"Oh thank you from the bottom of my heart! Right after that I loved to play the games girls would play and…you know being originally from the provinces it was hard for my parents to understand me and allow me to follow my inclinations and…"

He gets lost in the kind of explanations you find in romance novels and I get lost in my memories…

Girl's games? I played girl's games too. So what?

He's just spinning these yarns so that I'll feel sorry for him, for his sad fate and try to understand and console him.

Everybody is the same and wants to feel sorry for himself and go on moaning about his own fate. They need to create excuses and justifications for themselves, for their passions, their vices, their failures.

I also played girl's games, I did and what of it? I played them almost every Sunday with my little cousin who used to come and spend the afternoons with me.

"Julien, shall we play with dolls?"

"No, Michele I'd rather play Mommy and Daddy."

"Or we could play doctor, that's easier since you are sick, you're really sick aren't you? My parents always say I have to be nice to you because you are sick.

"No, at Mommy and Daddy."

"All right! But to make it more fun I'll be the Daddy and you'll be the Mommy."

"If you want, ok."

Dear sweet Michele what happened to you? You brought me so much joy!

My little Corsican cousin. I used to wait for those Sundays with such trepidation. You were almost joy in a world filled with terror. Michele you didn't know what I was thinking or even what I was, you were just satisfied being a child in a world of drastic changes.

I am twelve and I understand, I am the only one who understands…the others want to forget this world where our lives, our very existence is being questioned out of cowardice, laziness and ignorance. They all make believe they don't understand.

Where shall we go, we the forgotten ones of decolonization? Where is our home?

In France? In Italy? In Israel? Where? Where?

We Jews, are left behind, and ignored, in the panic that soon takes hold of everyone, everywhere... The Arabs hate us and are now the masters in their own country, what will they do to us? Are we to become second class citizens? Just like we treated them before?

The French despise us, the Israelis have nothing in common with us...they are all Russian, Polish, German Jews.

I hear them speaking in the living room, they believe in nothing, see nothing, live in rejection, in denial. After all, they proclaim with self satisfaction that we are at home here, we have made this country what it is, we have been here for generations and I hear them comment, agree, reassure themselves, even that moron Carmelo ventures an opinion. They're blabbering just as they did with the Nazis in 1939 and they all ended up in a camp....but the Germans in Tunis didn't have the time to be completely German...They quickly occupied the country with no real attempt on the part of the French or the Arabs to stop them, they set up forced labor teams, confiscated property, took hostages, proceeded with extortion of all kinds. They imposed the wearing of the yellow star and started committees headed by Jews to enforce the Nazi laws.

Actually, the Arabs and their leader the Great Bey are pleased by the turn of events... And the Grand Rabbi of Tunis is in the same position as every grand rabbi in the world, he pleads, he supplicates, intrigues, buys, protects his own friends, sells off his enemies, in one word he tries to get out of the mess. During that moment of fear and disarray the Jews are wondering what is happening to them, after all they are Tunisians and don't understand why they are being treated as Jews and as enemies, they don't get it... A round up is organized, the Germans under the approving eyes of the Arabs, place the Jews in camps and asked the Italians and their allies after all, to stand guard. The irony was that the Italians in Tunisia were our cousins, our friends or our servants…Some of them took their revenge because of their status as servants, friends, or cousins. A few less cooperative Jews are deported, others are killed in the name of Teutonic civilization. Just when the Germans finally decided to act like Germans and get rid of that disgusting race of troublemakers, the Allies arrived, but things came very close, and we almost… But it was just a reprieve, we were now in a country that had opened its eyes and realized what it is or wishes to be, and is filled with hatred and rancor for those who betrayed, who became almost French and who had forgotten their origins. The danger is there, ready to explode in our face?

So wake up! Do something! …

Dad, do something ! And Dad did something.

One morning he left to go to Paris with Fabien on a plane, with just a suitcase, like two thieves, like Polish Jews while I was somewhere clse wandering around in the world, trying to become a man. It was an easy trip, everyone is very nice to the Jewish immigrants, they arrive in Paris, start another shitty kind of life and then Mom joins them, and a little bit later, almost imme-diately… Smack, the rabbit punch came suddenly….

And then Dad and then…

We should have remained in Tunis… No that would have been worse, we would have become the victims of our victims, so what?

What? ….. Who wants us?

The old beau interrupts my daydreaming with another stupid question:

"So what do you think about it? I'm asking you, you seem totally absent."

"Not at all, I'm listening to you."

"So what do you think about it?"

"I understand you perfectly."

His burning eyes are shining and he smiles. Poor bastard! I can't help thinking that he's really pitiful.

"Thank you, thank you so much."

"Don't mention it!"

"You're eating very quickly, you must be very hungry!"

He continues with his blathering in an attempt to impress me and I plunge back to my dreams.

His hand drifted on to my knee, just like that, absent-mindedly, without much fanfare, he keeps on eating with his hand on my knee… But what gives him the right to put his hand on my knee? Where does he get that prerogative? Soon will he want to feed me as well?

Will he lift a fork full of meat and ask me to open my mouth? Just like Pina did when she fed me?

Pina sits me down on the kitchen table, the red table in the red kitchen. Pina, my maid, excuse me, no actually she was my governess—it sounds more upscale—who for ten years washed and fed me while she would teach me all about nursery rhymes: "sticks and stones…" and the other common sense words of that nursery rhyme. She made me repeat them so much that I ended up hating them.

"Open your mouth!"

"Close your mouth!"

"Chew your food!"

"Swallow!"

That's how my meals take place as I am sitting on the red table in the red kitchen, red, red like the blood of the bulls that are killed in the ring.

And in the living room I can hear my Dad and Fabien laughing and my mother also laughing much too loudly at everything that son of bitch Carmelo is saying.

"Open your mouth!"

A banderole, and some bright red blood, Olé! Olé! The crowd is screaming in the dining room.

"Close your mouth!"

A second banderole, the red kitchen, undercooked red meat in my mouth, "Viva el Toro" yells my mother, Carmelo must have put his hand on her thighs like this old man, with his hand on my knee.

Chew! Swallow! The thrust of the sword! I'm sinking, I'm dying, I can feel the red blood in the red kitchen that's going down my throat.

No! No! I don't want anymore, Dad! Dad! Help me! They're killing me and the bull doesn't want to be sacrificed. I hurt from the pain! I don't want to eat alone anymore, I want to be with you, I can't even get off the table if you don't come and get me; they just sat me there and they will leave me here and I'm afraid of being in the red kitchen. I start screaming: Dad! Dad! Come here, here!

"That child can be so temperamental, it's really hard to take—says my mother to her darling Carmelo; we must put a stop to his whimsical ideas. Of course I know one must be forgiving but after all there are limits. We can't even have lunch in peace and quiet."

My father comes into the kitchen.

"What's the matter, Julien, you know that we're having company!"

"Dad, I don't want to eat in the kitchen anymore, it scares me, it's so red!"

"All right, please let's discuss it this afternoon after lunch, okay? Stay quiet and I promise I'll do something about it. Come on be reasonable, be a good boy!"

Quiet? Quiet! Reasonable? Reasonable?

When I have the bull's blood in my mouth. Blood quiet, quiet, blood.

"But Daddy, no, no, I don't want to stay seated on this table like a wooden soldier."

"Now, now! Enough, you're exaggerating! Pina please, have him finish his lunch."

Dad, you too are betraying me! And I thought you were on my side against them all! Can't you see that Carmelo that Italian asshole who looks like Raf Vallone is nothing but a dog drooling after mother. Don't you give a damn or what? Do something, make him leave, throw him out! But no, I can hear you laughing just as mother who chortles every time he says something…

The old beau is also chuckling. He takes me by the elbow and whispers:

"So all my life was spent dreaming of Peter Pan."

"Have you ever been scared?" I ask him.

"Yes, of course."

"But I mean very, very frightened."

"Yes, I think so."

"Are you sure of it?"

"Why do you insist so much?"

"Because I feel it's important to have been very scared."

"You know you're very intelligent, so engaging. I am very happy to have met you."

"Thank you, that's very nice, you seem to understand people very well."

"I try to guess and then to establish friendly relations, an understanding and perhaps later... Would you like a chocolate ice cream? You look so dreamy."

"I'd like to know whether there is any connection between chocolate ice cream and someone who looks dreamy."

"Have you seen Bergman's latest film? What do you think of it?"

"Nothing."

"What do you mean nothing? Do you think I should go and see it?"

"Fabien, just do what you want."

"But I'm not Fabien, my name is Richard."

"..."

"Richard, do you hear me? Richard!"

"Yes, yes, Richard, Richard, Richard, excuse me."

"You are very strange you know!"

"Yes I know that, I am very strange, more than you'll ever know."

A long silence. He's drinking his Bordeaux absent-mindedly as if he were trying to find the next topic of conversation.

I never went back to the rue Pierre Demours or the rue Lebon... I do everything I can to avoid those two streets... The ironies of life are simply hallucinating, even I, couldn't have invented anything like it rue Lebon ? The "Good Street"?

That's where my parents landed in Paris, after running away from Tunis. It was in a small two-bit storefront where Mom, Dad, and Fabien were selling olives and Judeo-Tunisian food to French people who treated them as though they were Arabs, or pieds-noirs, or just some poor ghetto Jews.

Mother, who used to spend her time at the hairdresser and in antique shops, is now cooking all day; she makes couscous and tajins that she sells to real French people; Dad is holding his head in his hands in the kitchen; and Fabien makes the rounds of the outdoor fritter vendors in Paris who are all Arabs to try and sell them olive oil.

They live in humiliation, shame, the shame and the fear of what tomorrow will bring.

But now they're in France, they're free, they're not afraid of the Arabs anymore, they're all right, they're happy or at least almost happy. As a child I never asked myself the question whether or not I hated the Arabs, they were part of our everyday lives, they lived with us, in our home. I can't remember ever hearing my parents say "dirty Arab" or anything like that... We were like cousins who understood each other without having to speak, never eager to show too much affection but never harboring any real hatred either. Perhaps because they were seen as inferior to us? I can't tell... Dad always treated the Arabs with respect; he could speak Arabic and was a Jewish Arab, something that may be hard to understand but that did exist... But once they fled Tunis to go to Paris everything changed. In France we are humiliated; we are an underclass so now everything is the fault of the Arabs; we were forced to hate them … and very, very quickly, they realize that the same Arabs were also living in Paris with the same Jews and that they have the same problems… No, here in Paris it's much worse. Here we've become like Arabs and the real French people consider us as Arabs too, and they despise us. The real French people are worse than the Arabs; no, that's not fair to say. We should be thankful to the French for having accepted us in their beautiful, demo-cratic and republican country, France—where they say—we have become first class citizens and where we can benefit from the great Western culture.

Richard is still touching my arm.

"Have you already been told that you a rebel?"

"Yes I've been told many times, too many, in fact. I'm getting tired of hearing the same deep things said about me over and over!"

"I can feel that you have suffered a lot!"

"Oh yes! That's something really new. I never heard that kind of comment before and I'm at a loss for some original remark. 'Please don't touch my wounds that haven't yet healed.' That's from Chekhov or perhaps Racine, no it's in Gogol. I can't remember anymore."

"I'd love to see you laugh and make jokes!"

"Me too."

"Me too, what?"

"I'd like to see myself laughing and making jokes."

Richard gets up, buttons his shirt collar and straightens his tie around his bull neck that now appears really crimson after eating all that red meat, or perhaps it's my presence that makes him grow red all the way up to his throat and face.

He adds shyly and in a childish voice:

"You know, I'm very sorry, but I must go. I hope to see you again soon. Time has gone by so quickly in your company that I didn't get to tell you the whole story and I have so many more things to share with you. Here's my phone number. I hope to hear from you."

He hands me a business card with his name: Richard Benoit.

"Good bye, Richard."

He leaves without turning around; he walks with a heavy gait and seems much older. He doesn't look like Fabien anymore but like a poor man devastated by loneliness. I suddenly feel very sorry for him and I want to call him back and console him as if he were my grandfather.

I hope I never see him again, I have no wish to humiliate him any further; he's just as lonely as I am.

The restaurant where you can have the best meat in Paris is continuously filling up; people come and go and stuff themselves with gigantic mouthfuls of very red meat and then guzzle down glass upon glass of red wine and then they wonder why they get heart attacks. I take pleasure in watching the people sitting all around me, the obese and the diabetics they will all become in the future. Richard paid the bill and left the restaurant. At another table there's a woman sitting and staring at me intensely; she smiles at me; she's in the company of another Richard. She looks just like Cléo but so much that I could swear it is Cléo herself.

Cléo… Cléo, the little French can-can dancer at the Folies Bergère.

Monique says that we were all drunk that night, but I never get drunk. My father taught me that we Jews never get drunk, one more silly idea I almost believed in. Monique calls me: she wants to see me again: "Come to the usual club after one in the morning, I must work before one, I have a surprise for you."

I reach the Mandarin at five minutes past one… Eight splendid six foot tall fillies are with Monique, all of them dancers from the Folies Bergère, very excited to have their first evening of true freedom for the twenty first birthday of one of them.

Cléo really wants to celebrate her birthday and take advantage of one evening off.

A true dream-like creature, with the body of a warrior, an Amazon, as hard as marble, an angelic-looking face framed by locks of blonde hair like a Botticelli painting and a sweet and docile mouth. But at the club and in public I stop at the limits of heavy petting. Monique insists that we should all go to her place only three streets away.

Cléo disappears into the bathroom and comes out a few minutes later naked and draped in a bedspread; she sits at my feet; I'm holding a scraper that ends in an eagle's claw. I caress her body with my claw and penetrate into her most intimate parts, her breast, her thighs, her greatest intimacies that have no further secrets left for me to explore. The others laugh and make some comments. Monique is blushing with pleasure …

Cléo stands up slowly and unveils her entire body while the others give a round of applause...

Cléo comes up to me, takes my hands and places them on her naked breasts then she kneels in front of me... Monique and another can-can girl are locked in a deep French kiss, while two others disappear into the bedroom...

Cléo leads me by the hand to the sofa in the living room ...the others gather around...

Did all this really happen? Even I can't tell anymore. I don't exactly know what is true and what is not but none of it is that important... What is important is... I don't know, I can't tell anymore, I never did know. The Cleo in the restaurant is still looking at me and smiling while her Richard blathers away ... a voice startles me.

"Would you like another cup of coffee?"

"No, thank you. I'm fine. "

"Are you sure?"

The waiter is standing in front of the table looking bored and inquisitive... I feel the urgent need to say something.

"So now we're not allowed to dream, right? Right?"

"Excuse me?"

"No, nothing."

That asshole flunkey interrupted my dream; he looks at me without moving, without uttering a single word, with that bored look of his... I think I have to leave, there are people standing up in front of me waiting for my table. I get up slowly, put my leather jacket back on and push away my chair while the waiter who doesn't miss a beat says mockingly, looking at me straight in the eyes, "Goodbye sir, thank you very much."

I leave the restaurant thinking about Cléo or Louise or Katia, Eliane, Catherine, Dominique, Anne Marie, Noelle, Anne, Linda, Janine, Margaret, Michèle, Danièle …

And…all the others…

It's now two-thirty in the afternoon and a whole day ahead of me without a fucking thing to do; it's going to be long…

I feel like smoking a cigar! I can afford to buy one since I was just offered an entire free meal, and more than just one, two! With all the food I ingurgitated at lunch I can skip dinner tonight. I go into a "café tabac" with a self-important attitude. I walk up to the counter of the smoke shop and ask out loud the old wicked witch sitting behind the counter who looks like the perfect caricature of a concierge.

"A cigar! I'd like a Robt. Burns please!"

She hands me a whole box of cigars with a condescending little smile.

"That'll be five francs seventy-five."

"No, madam, just one, a loose cigar."

The bitch! I'm convinced she did it on purpose to humiliate me; she's staring at me.

"Thank you, madam, goodbye madam!"

That's funny, when I buy just one cigar, I get the urge to be so polite, so humble!

I have the feeling that I need to excuse myself for asking for a single cigar!

Like poor people must feel! Even when they pay their bills they excuse themselves, they want to be forgiven for being poor!

I'm look forward to the day when I'll be rich!

Rich and important, rich and respected, rich and therefore handsome in the eyes of the entire world.

As I think about it I feel like laughing, singing, dancing, being happy, happy even for a single minute, and I want to forget, to take the risk of being disliked, I don't give a damn, I want to be myself! I want to say whatever I'm thinking regardless of the consequences. I want to go to a smoke shop and say "Give me a pack of tobacco, the cheapest kind" without giving a shit about the ten people around me who are looking at me with a knowing smile. I want to say aloud whatever I'm thinking.

I'm so bold suddenly it must be the red Bordeaux or the red meat or the Fabien old beau with his red neck.

The one thing that makes me speechless is when I encounter utter stupidity... I much prefer meanness to stupidity but the world is filled with stupid people and assholes dominate society.

I stop one of them in the street.

"Sir, are you aware of being an asshole?"

"Excuse me?"

"No, no, nothing."

I approach a second one.

"Sir, do you know that you are an asshole?"

"..."

"Sir, do you know that you are an asshole?"

"You must be drunk!"

"Me? Not at all."

"Well, in that case you're crazy!"

"Oh! Oh! Oh!"

I'm having lots of fun. Let's try one more.

"Sir, are you aware of being an asshole?"

"Yes, definitely, and you?"

The bastard caught me at my own game!

I don't feel like laughing anymore or saying whatever the hell I'm thinking. I feel like…I feel like looking at something beautiful! Or maybe doing something useful, even useful to other people—that'll be a change for me.

Lillian, why are we seeing each other again, huh? Tell me! Why do you spend two hours with me from time to time? Because you want to get screwed? I'm not interested in becoming the one who screws. I have some dignity left in me, after all!

Your punishment will be no more me screwing you! Even though I feel like it. In any case I'm convinced that you'll find someone else easily enough and quickly enough.

You always find someone to console yourself with. It's part of human nature: we can't be alone, we need someone to justify our insecurity, our cowardice and actually women are just as lonely as we are, even more so, as they watch themselves get older, melting away like an old candle, losing it all, losing everything that was still beautiful and trying desperately to fight it….

Even my aunt with the laughing thighs couldn't stay by herself. A few years ago I met her in the street and she threw herself in my arms and whispered in my ear:

"It's been so long. What are you up to?"

"I'm here, I'm working, I'm an actor now."

"Oh, really? That sounds wonderful. We should meet and talk. To discuss what's going on with you. I haven't seen you since your father's funeral. Will you come over for lunch at my place, say Thursday afternoon? I haven't seen you in so long."

"But this is the first invitation I get from you. No one in the family invites me, my dear aunt!"

"Don't call me 'my dear aunt.'"

"Well, you'd rather I call you 'Tata'"?

"Oh no, it makes me feel as if I were seventy years old!"

"And how old are you?"

"I turned forty-three the day before yesterday!"

"Well you don't look your age at all. You've been through so much, you look at least…fifty…no, I'm joking…you look very young."

"And you are so mature."

"Mature for what?"

"So are you OK for Thursday? For lunch!"

"Yes I'll be there, we'll get to know each other, we know each other so little, it's a shame, don't you think?"

"Yes it's a shame."

"We only met once when my Dad died, when he was buried, do you remember? You were sitting in front of me and it was so hot, and you were feeling so hot."

"Oh yes, your poor father, he was such a marvelous brother to me. Thursday we'll talk about all that. Good, so I'll see you then?"

"I warn you that we shall only talk."

"Of course, yes what else? Listen, I'll see you Thursday, OK? You agree, you will come, won't you?"

"Fine, but I warned you."

Poor woman, what happened in the hearse wasn't enough for her. She must have been waiting for me for a long time. She probably put some rouge on her cheeks, mascara around her eyes, green over her eyelids, white cream everywhere else, covered her body with perfume, even the most intimate parts.

She must have changed her dress ten times in front of a mirror as old as she is...

She is waiting for me, and slowly, the rouge fades away, the mascara starts dripping, the green shadow is running, the white cream turns grey, the dress that had been changed ten times is totally crumpled and even the mirror is cloudy.

She looks at her watch and goes into the kitchen for a glass of water.

She's no longer expecting me, and she sits on a straight back chair and she becomes once more a Jewish mother without a child; she contemplates her own solitude, lamenting her fate as a woman who is now a widow and is inevitably getting older. Her husband died during the war in Algeria; she never remarried, to honor his memory, but mostly out of fear of the unknown, and now she doesn't know how to handle her loneliness and boredom... Perhaps she really does have desires; maybe she really does have needs to fulfill. Who knows? She waits and hopes but is too fearful to act and to find someone.

She waits for me, and waits...

When someone is waiting for me, I feel I exist, it makes me feel alive, they wait for me because they want to see me and it really gives me a certain pleasure.

As for me I hate waiting and yet I'm always arriving at my appointments way in advance; everywhere I go or have to go, I'm always there one hour ahead of time, running around in circles, practically like a dog biting its tail. I think I know where that comes from: when I had my bad legs it always took me an incredible amount of time to go anywhere and keep my appointments. I had to leave two hours ahead of time it always took me so long to reach a given location. I'd drag myself there and made it no matter what because I needed to see other people. The habit stayed with me…to be everywhere ahead of time.

But damn!

What's happening to me? Why am I all alone for days and weeks on end. Am I depressed? Am I, as they say, sinking into a deep depression?

I know that I hate being alone and yet I spend entire days without seeing anyone. What's happening to me? I don't feel like seeing anybody, I'm self-sufficient. Maybe if I jerked off less I would need to be with other people more. I don't get it. I find that everybody is stupid, uninteresting, worthless, and limited… I'm either crazy or a genius or maybe just a pretentious little depressed asshole. So how long is it going to take for me to get some recognition? How marvelous I will be toward everyone; I'll remain so simple, I'll be such a normal person or almost normal. To some I shall be the great Jewish actor, since they say such a category does exist, by the way. Me? The great Jewish actor? If they hadn't constantly reminded me that I was Jewish I would have certainly forgotten it…

"He's a Jew!"

"I know he is."

"How do you know?"

"I just do."

"And as your mother I forbid you to date a Jew and spend anytime with him? With a Jew!!"

If she only knew that I can hear every word she's saying from the parlor because the flunky blocked my way in and made sure I stayed at the door… me her Jewish university buddy …!

Who could even imagine that such attitudes could still exist in France at that time…or even these days… I am a Jew, a good Jew, a different Jew, an assimilated Jew but still a Jew in any case. Whatever the politics, or the problems may be, it's always our fault, we are the ones who benefit, who disturb, who prevent things from running smoothly, the murderers of the Christian god, both the creators and the victims of communism. Soon every Muslim in the world will hate us and want to exterminate us.

All day the graffiti everywhere are attacking me and reminding me that I am a Jew!

Nice: reopen the Ovens! Death to the Kikes!

Sentier metro station: Jews to the gas chambers!

Strasbourg: Let's burn the synagogue to the ground.

Israel = Nazi.

And taxi drivers lose their cool behind a delivery van marked LEVY and scream "Filthy Jew!"

"But mother I assure you he's really wonderful."

"I have no doubt that he's intelligent. Those people are all very smart, or at least they are cunning."

"But mother, besides being intelligent I can tell you he's a very nice person."

"What? What do you mean 'Besides his intelligence?' Did he Jew you up sexually as well? My poor child what will become of you?"

At that point I could no longer wait quietly at the door and I moved in and pushed the cleaning woman aside. I opened the door leading into the parlor of the magnificent apartment on the avenue de la Grande Armée and like a brave soldier of Napoleon I said:

"Excuse me, madam, the little intelligent Jew would like to say a few words. I never screwed your daughter because I would have had the feeling of screwing you, which is an unbearable thought. To tell you the truth I haven't even put my hand in her crotch even though she wants me to do it passionately. You may rest in peace! You can be sure that your daughter hasn't been defiled at the hand of a Jew. Good night, madam, good night, Sylvie, may God bless you and watch over you and all those French people from old and honorable families, may God watch over your ancestors who have made this country what it is, an ocean of pretense and prejudice..."

I was really wonderful that day! All the world's Jews must have jumped for joy and to sing my praise. Only a few non-Jews and the self-hating Jews are still saying that there is no more anti-Semitism in France.

In any case I didn't feel like going out with Sylvie that much. With my father sick in the hospital, how can I be thinking of going out with her? If at least I was screwing her, but no, not even, the well-bred young lady will fuck with a Jew. We hold hands, talk about literature, go to the movies, kiss a little, touch each other a bit above the waist or below the thighs but no fucking. In any case, when your father is sick and dying, we shouldn't think about any of this petting, it's just obscene; when your father is in the hospital you must suffer and can't just go on living as before, don't you think?

You can only live in slow motion, you must stop wanting to laugh, to drink, to tell jokes, to touch girls, to caress Sylvie, or do anything else, anything. You can only feel guilty because your father is dying.

Had I known the rest of it I wouldn't have been so sarcastic; one week later I was writing Sylvie that my father had died that night… I was also telling her that I really didn't want to see her or even hear from her. Another life was beginning for me. I wanted to go ahead in my desire to be in the theater and I couldn't waste my time with her kind of society people… As a souvenir, Sylvie, I send you the description of my father's final moments, someone your family must clearly despise because he is a Jew.

The 25th—my father died last night at one in the morning; on Monday afternoon at four I was at home listening to Hungarian dances by Brahms. My sister-in-law came to pick me up. She cried out from downstairs in the street: "Julien, Julien, come quickly, hurry, your father is getting much worse, and he's got very little time left."

During the taxi ride on the way to the hospital at Asnières what was I thinking about? I can't remember... I kept on looking out the window of the car at the trees in the Bois de Boulogne whipping by.

I have no memories, just a huge void moment, a big hole, a chasm. As we reached the hospital I see a bed where a man I can't even recognize has been thrown, it's my father: a plastic tube is dangling from his nose down into a glass container laying on the floor, a second plastic tube goes from his arm to a bottle red with blood that is dripping down slowly, drop by drop. His face is grey, I can only see the whites of his eyes that are covered with a yellowish substance; his body that had appeared to be so bloated lately now seems so tiny under the ivory white sheets.

He's still conscious and sees me and says:

"I'm sorry, Julien!"

Sorry? Sorry about what?

Five people are around his bed: my mother, who looks as though she's thinking about what she's going to have for dinner this evening; my grandmother, who seems to be thinking about what her daughter will have for dinner that evening; my father's brother, who must be pondering the problems he'll have at work tomorrow and his professional responsibilities should my father die during the night; my sister-in-law, who is looking at me and remains silent; and then me.

And I am looking for someone who should be there: where is he? Why isn't he here? He should be present on such an occasion. His place is here.

Where is Fabien?

My brother, where is my brother? He should be here to help me, next to me but he's not here; he died a stupid death... Smack! Whiplash... Smack!

The doctor comes by and tells us that it will happen during the night. I feel nothing when he says it, not even pity. My father falls asleep after they give him a shot of morphine. We decide to spend the night at his bedside, my sister-in-law, my mother, and myself. After about one hour my mother and sister-in-law fall asleep. I stay awake at my father's bedside as he falls into a long delirium; it's now early dawn. During the night the nurse came to check his blood pressure, which is excellent at 130; his heart is holding up very well.

Tuesday 8 a.m.

I go downstairs to get a cup of coffee; my mother and Claudia went home to get some sleep and I went back inside his room at 8:30 a.m. My father is basically out of his coma and is looking at me with his huge and intelligent eyes. He wants me to recite the prayer "Shema Israel." Me? How could I recite the "Shema Israel" prayer since I don't even know it and have never learned it. I haven't heard it in an eternity... Well in any case I'll pretend, I'll just mumble something; I'm sure that at that specific instant he won't even figure out what I'm saying, so it's not that important...

And then he cries as he asks me to forgive him... Forgive? Forgive what? For what? And then I start looking at him deeply. I see him as the companion of my childhood, the one who played hide and seek with me, the one who wrestled with me, the one who hugged me, who was saying that I was the strongest of them all, and who was such a bad liar.

"Hey Dad, I'm the strongest."

"It's true. You're really tough!"

"Dad help me, tell me that someday I'll be able to run, to dance, to dance through the sky just like Peter Pan, tell me that, Dad, say it to me!"

I understand...that I never stopped loving him even though I wanted to lose him for five years and I tell him.

Large manly tears run down his sunken cheeks that are disappearing and he regrets that he is leaving me nothing when he's actually leaving me his love. He falls asleep and I fall asleep with him.

Noon

I'm awakened by his dry and rough cough; he's throwing up blood, pints of blood, and I'm holding the bowl where his life is winding itself down; large black clots of blood are running and running uninterruptedly and are mixed with my tears; then, exhausted, he stops and falls back into a semi-coma.

The doctor comes by at that time and tells me it's best that I don't leave the room, that it may only be a matter of hours or maybe even minutes. I panic when I hear it's imminent and call the family, who come by two hours later; they're all surprised to see that I'm still there. I, the disowned one, the one who left home, the bad son who loved freedom, who wants to be an actor, they're surprised to see me so calm and so quiet. I, calm and quiet? If only they knew what was going on inside me... If they only knew. They will never know; we don't belong to the same world; it would be useless to try and explain; they wouldn't understand.

My father lifts his arm and lets it fall in a sign of powerlessness over and over for about one hour. Everyone else around me is crying. I am not crying. Between my father and myself there is a pact, a pact of love. I feel him with me and I feel his heart inside mine. The others look at each other and elbow each other to point out my dry eyes as a sign that I have no feelings. The doctor comes in and says there is internal hemorrhaging due to a perforation of the stomach: more and more blood transfusions, the blood keeps on dripping from the bottle into his arm. At 6 p.m. my father suddenly is again conscious and awake and repeats to me everything he said regarding his final wishes. The others all suddenly jump at the opportunity and decide, given the circumstances, that I'm the only one who can spend another night at his bedside. They leave the room as quickly as possible to go back to their homes.

And now I am alone with him.

The nurses make their continuous rounds and repeat that his blood pressure is very good and that they have never seen such a strong heart. As I sit next to him I remember all those nights when he would sit next to my bed and tell me stories where I appeared as the indestructible hero. He never reminds me of my condition even though he, too, hears what people are saying. Those words that still haunt me.

"He'll never make it."

"Yes, he will, you'll see."

"He won't make it."

"You'll see, he will."

"Won't make it."

"Yes, you'll see."

"Won't make it."

"You'll see…"

"Won't…"

"We'll see…"

It's an awful night. I have to hold his hand because he's trying to pull the tubes out of his nose because it bothers him terribly; he's suffering and there's nothing I can do, just pathetically mop his forehead that's streaming with tears and sweat. He's suffering and I can only be sleepy; he's in agony and I can only feel back pain.

"Help me Dad, help me! I still need you, even now you must help me endure your suffering, and you were always so good at doing things for others and for me. Even when you're dying you must help me… I'm scared Dad… I'm scared…"

I'm scared… I recapture the fear of my childhood that I had forgotten…the fear that would freeze me up when they left me alone.

They all went out and I stayed behind.

They left me with my crutches near my bed. "You'll be able to get up if you need to go to the bathroom."

Thank you for the delicate thought.

They all went away and left me there, leaving me like a dog tied to a leash.

"In any case he can't go very far" My legs are my leash. I'm afraid… I hate Saturday nights, when the servants have their night off, as though servants needed one… Pfft! Day off? To do what? Movies, a girlfriend, to go for a walk, go dancing see the parents; they work like dogs all week and to enjoy their day off, they dress up with incredible bad taste, the kind of bad taste only cleaning ladies can think of and they go out on Saturday nights...!

And I'm scared....

And my parents go out on Saturday nights, just like the maid, to play bridge; well I'd like to stick their bridge up somewhere!

"Dad you'll leave the light on in the doorway, right? Don't forget!"

"Yes, yes, of course."

I can't even get up to check that he didn't forget. I don't even have the guts because I would have to walk through the long, long hallway. It's so hard being a cripple, to be thirteen, to be alone and scared on a Saturday night in a big, a very big "beautiful house." The hall must be more than one hundred and fifty feet long! It'll take me over five minutes to get through it on my crutches...

Five minutes of being scared stiff is too long! What do I do if the phone rings? Do I answer it or don't I answer it? If I get up to answer I have to cross the entire living room because the phone is at the other end of the room, sitting on the table like a big white worm, so by the time I reach it, the ringing will have stopped.

A white telephone! How stupid can they be to think it makes them look richer!...A bunch of jerks!

If I don't answer the thieves who are calling to see if anyone is home will conclude that the house is empty and will come around to rob us. What do I do then?

I'll try to fall asleep very quickly, as quickly as possible, to get to tomorrow morning in five minutes. I am more and more scared. I try to go to sleep but cries come out of my throat and the sound of my crying fills the room.

I'm so fuckin' tired of being a cripple!

And my brother could at least stay home on Saturday nights. Instead he goes to the Hot Jazz Club to listen to jazz! How absurd! He thinks he's Louis Armstrong. I hear noises in the kitchen. I'm sure there's someone there! So what do I do? Do I cry out or keep quiet?

If I yell he'll come running over to kill me, but if I keep quiet he'll also come to search every room. So?

Yes, this time I'm sure there's someone in the kitchen. I clearly hear the steps! How late can it be? Ten, nine, eleven o'clock…? I didn't even think of asking for an alarm clock; they could have given it some thought after all!

No I'm just imagining things, there's nobody, it's incredible what fear will do to you! You go on imagining silly things that can't happen or only happen in movies.

"Mommy, what if the doorbell rings?"

"If it rings don't you answer it!"

Easier said than done—don't answer—was she ever alone in a house?

Did she ever hear the doorbell ring many times, non-stop, one night alone in the house! Does she know that every ring makes your blood curdle, crushes your bones, and your hair stand up?

I'm afraid.

I'm afraid of being afraid.

I'm ashamed of being afraid of being afraid.

I feel like peeing.

Let's cool it and think of happy, funny things, but… I have nothing, I find nothing.

But why did I take a nap this afternoon? It's obviously the reason I'm not sleepy now.

"Come on, you have to take a nap."

"I'm not sleepy."

"But you must. It'll give you strength."

Strength? What for?

In any case I'm lying down. I'm always lying down.

They don't know what to do with me, so they tell me that I have to take a nap.

The wall facing my bed is blue. I never did notice how cruel the color blue can be.

There are spots on the wall that look like mean men. They look at me and laugh and make fun of me.

I'm afraid.

They'll wind up coming out of the wall and surrounding my bed showing me big snakes. I must ignore them, otherwise they'll get angry.

OK, let me close my eyes... Yes but if I close my eyes I won't see them getting closer and once they are near my bed they'll strangle me or they'll want to look at my fanny or even touch it.

"If you think you're scaring me, you're nothing but spots on the wall."

I'm scared… But why did they leave me alone? And soon it will be next Saturday and I'll be all alone again.

I'm scared Daddy, I'm scared… Your breathing is almost peaceful. You're asleep and I'm looking at the

blue wall in the hospital room. You must help me overcome my fear, you must help me endure your suffering,
even if you die, even if you die, help me Dad, help me.
Only if you help me will I be able to get through this,
you must, you must... Dad? Dad? You're not saying
anything, there's nothing you can do for me anymore, I
need you so much. You see I'm closing my eyes I'm
going to doze off in my armchair while you're in your
white bed. I close my eyes, I don't want to dream, and I
slowly fade away ...

I hear screams that seem to come from a crib left in
the middle of a field... It's very hot, a stifling kind of
heat, that grabs me by the throat, but strangely I also feel
the drops of a cold sweat dripping down my back, my
hips and between my legs... My legs, and my thighs
especially hurt so much. I exercised too much yesterday,
the muscles ache and are swollen as they bulge through
my pants... I try to get closer to the crib, the field has
turned into a sort of no man's land of sand and bushes
and a tiny stream of black water which emanates an
awful smell of pestilence and putrefaction, flows down
the middle. It becomes harder and harder to go forward;
the black stream is really a sewer and all kinds of
garbage and waste are floating on its surface, orange
peels, date pits, empty cans, a bone, a clump of hair, a
book with block letters saying "It is forbidden to come
closer."

I attempt to open the book but I can't, there's a sort
of hand pulling in the opposite direction to keep the book
closed... I pull so hard with both my hands that it finally
opens with the same noise as a huge door. Inside the

book I see a woman lying down who is looking at me smiling; she is naked and very skinny, her empty breasts are dangling on her chest, she has no teeth, and she is licking her lips with a red and very pointed tongue like a viper. Suddenly she opens her legs and a huge black hole appears as if to devour me. I turn my head away so as not to look but I still see her face, her eyes roll out of their sockets and fall to the bottom of the book that closes up once again.

The cries coming from the crib have turned into sobs and muffled moans and the crib seems to be still so far away. I must go down the slope into a gully and climb up slowly; my aching thighs tell me to catch my breath but I keep going forward, forward even more. At the bottom of the black hole I see the crib, the cries have stopped and lowering my face I can distinguish lying down on a multicolored blanket what looks like a tiny body hidden by a white sheet.

There is nothing moving, not a sound is coming from the crib now, but the sounds of crickets all around and the sound of the sun. I hear the voices of both men and women mumbling at a distance, all speaking at once. I can't make out what they are saying.

There is a little musical ditty coming from the crib now, a rhyme that repeats the same sad notes over and over again. The voices are coming closer, a mixture of French, Arabic, and German; a few Italian words are thrown in at times… A crowd of people appears suddenly at the top of the hill, they are all running in every direction as if to escape an unknown threat; they run, fall and get back up; they're dressed in black with yellow emblems on their clothes. But who are these people? Why are they running so fast, why are they falling? What are they afraid of? They all disappear at the bottom of the hill, swallowed by the earth that opens up. Everything is quiet once again, even the crickets and the sun are now silent... The body under the white sheet seems to have grown, and it's very odd...

I start walking again and the crib is following me. Actually it's fastened to my feet with a rope and I'm having trouble pulling it; it's heavier and heavier... But who is under that sheet?

Three people are following me I can't see their faces; they're walking with their faces turned down and are chanting an incessant litany. But who are they? They overtake me and vanish into the blue sea.

The sand makes it hard for me to go forward and the sand is getting hotter and hotter and I can feel it burning through the soles of my shoes. I stop at the little black water stream. But why is the water so black? The three shadows that have been following me are in front of me now, smiling. I can't recognize who they are, they're speaking words I can't understand....they make gestures I can't see, but who are they? What are they expecting from me?

I try to go forward again but I can't anymore, the sand is too hot, my legs hurt too much, the sky is too blue, the sun is too high. I sit on the ground not too far from the crib.

But who is in that crib anyway, under the white sheet?

There is total silence now, not a sound, not a noise, not a whisper, nothing…nothing. The three shadows appear very close in front of me, I can almost touch them but I still don't see their faces; they surround the crib and are holding hands tightly and peacefully… But who are they?

I get up with great difficulty and fall to my knees and slowly I get closer to the crib…

But who is it in the crib under that white sheet?

I attempt to lift the sheet but it's so heavy, very heavy, as heavy as lead. The three shadows put their arms forward and start lifting the sheet and now I am able to recognize who they are: my brother Fabien, my father, and my mother are smiling… But why is my brother older than my parents who appear to be in their twenties? My brother's face has wrinkles on his face like an old man. How can this be possible?

They keep on lifting the lead-heavy sheet and I see my face as a child appearing smiling. I look so happy and begin to laugh softly; everyone is smiling…the sheet is lifted some more and it uncovers me. My parents and my brother are no longer smiling; their faces are now covered with tears; my body is now that of a man.

A man with a child's face… But how can this be possible? The sheet is now black and as I lean over closer to my crib I discover to my horror that my body stops at the knees and two stumps… I turn toward my father, but he has disappeared, they have all disappeared, I am alone in the middle of the desert with my stumps and I am screaming with horror…a high pitched scream comes out of my throat…

I'm startled out of my sleep. I open my eyes and sit on the edge of the armchair where I've been sleeping and I'm drenched in sweat and have even pissed all over myself. I must have been very scared during the night when I had my nightmare, this recurring nightmare that's been haunting me. It's always the same but it gets clearer and comes into greater focus, as if to tell me... It's not over yet, but soon.

Wednesday

His face is like that of a skeleton, he has the hiccups, he has black and purple circles around the eyes eating away at his face, his limbs are lifeless, his jet black hair is covered with white spots, the bones in his face are incredibly visible; the hemorrhaging has stopped. At ten in the morning the nurses come in to place a catheter into his penis to avoid any danger of uremia; he emerges from his coma to ask me to get him a few Tchaikovsky records and then falls back to sleep under the effects of morphine.

A second patient is placed in his room and he moans incessantly with the noises of an airplane taking off.

My father is destroyed by the struggle and the nurses are sure that the end will take place during the night.

I remain since I want to fulfill his final requests. One of the few things I could have done for him. The waiting is horrible, I am frightened, every noise inside the room takes on an incredible dimension, I feel cold, I hurt for him. The man dying next to him is screaming from the pain.

Thursday

He's still hanging on; his breathing is hoarse and cavernous. "Congested lungs." He has trouble breathing, says the doctor.

The whole family arrives, accompanied by a very religious uncle, a true believer who enters the room like the messiah. His arrival prompts me into an uncontrollable nervous and happy laughter that is unstoppable; people look at each other, shocked at my hard and pitilessly dry heart; they whisper among themselves but I don't hear what they're saying; only my father looks and smiles at me, as if he'd finally understood me after all those years I stayed away.

He gives me his hand that I squeeze eagerly as I go on laughing.

"It's horrible to see someone die," says my mother.
"We must pray," says the messiah.
"It's the end," says my uncle.
The others take out their handkerchiefs.

All we are missing are the professional criers to complete the spectacle. Every half hour my father regains consciousness for one or two minutes, only to whisper words such as "love" and "good health to all of you" or "I did what I could." Not once during his agony with a terrible and admirable lucidity did he say my brother's name and yet he revered him and his heart, that damn heart of his, kept on going.

Thursday night.

I'm alone with him once again and his eyes are now completely covered with a grey veil; his tongue, which is visible as he keeps his mouth open, is separating into bloody slices that are flaking away, his lips look like old parchment.

He's had nothing to eat since Sunday night and the red blood from the white bottle keeps on dripping through the plastic tube going into his arm that has now become entirely blue and seems to be separated from the rest of his body.

Julien...Julien...in the silence and the darkness of the night his whispers have awakened me... The hospital room is completely dark, his bed is barely illuminated by the outer darkness.

Julien...Julien ...he calls me quietly whispering... Julien...

I get up from my armchair and come closer to his bed... I lean over toward him, his eyes are wide open and he is repeating in a whisper:

"Julien... Julien ..."

"What is it, Dad? What?"

"Listen, listen..."

"What, Dad? What?"

"You wanted to know how it was over there?"

"Where, Dad, where?"

"Over there, over there...a long, a very long time ago, look...you see? You see?"

"Where, Dad?"

His face no longer shows signs of pain, he looks younger...and different...yes different.

There is terror on his face, unbearable terror, a green inescapable fear.

"Over there... Come here, closer to me, closer, closer."

He wants to whisper into my ear.

Over there it was...

I can't understand the words he's saying and he begins to shake, his whole body is shaking everywhere, his entire soul trembles and with his hand he draws circles in the air... He continues to whisper and I also begin trembling just like him...my whole body is shaking in the silence of the night punctuated by his incomprehensible whispering...

I can see on his face, in his lifeless eyes... I see in his fear...long barracks, electrified barbed wire fences, charnels, Germans, dogs, bodies cut to pieces, helmets, uniforms and shaved heads, bodies without bodies and he whispers and whispers without stopping... And on his face I can see clearly, distinctly... Bodies burning, contorting themselves, children saying nothing, looking sad, men who cry and piss in their pants, fall down and get up like automatons and moan and implore God and humanity... Death stinks and the odor is now unbearable, a stifling grey smell... The smell comes from him, he's still in the process of dying with them, he's dying for the hundredth time...and he whispers as he shakes and passes on to me the fear and the doubt and the strength and the hatred. I finally understand who he is. I understand this man at last whom I call my father, my father. He was 33 when he was put in that camp, one more martyr… How many martyrs were 33 years old?… How many were crucified for the love of the new race?

"Julien…that's how it was, don't forget, don't forget, don't forget…"

The shaking has stopped, his face has recaptured its pain, silence has returned, the black night has once more imposed its will, and I am here in his room, without a sigh or a word, without a flutter.

So I am here.

The son of the unknown man, the son of a poor corpse thrown on that bed, the son of the martyr… The son of the man I can now call my father.

"Don't forget, don't forget."

Friday morning

His blood pressure has suddenly dropped, his pulse is beating 170; he's nothing but an old rag in a bed that's much too big for him. He's breathing much faster with a whistling sound and more hoarsely than before.

He coughs and spits and I go and take the spit out of his throat with a cotton swab. He has one last instant of awareness and tells me:

"You were right, one shouldn't be fearful of life, grab as much of it as you can. You see I'm dying a happy man because inadvertently and due to my own foolishness I managed to make you become a man way before your time."

But what's he talking about? What foolishness?

Me, a grown man?

He asked me to kiss him and blessed me as he asked me to say "no" to the others because they had turned him away from me. He sank back into his coma with a smile on his face. The day goes by breathing with him, suffering with him, loving him with the others who are crying and the messiah who is praying.

He has this grin on one side of his face where three front teeth have fallen out, and I had this strange and proud feeling overtake me, I was proud of the man who could fight that way, who could lay there with his sad look but who also appeared to be challenging everyone...

Don't forget, don't forget... Now I know how it was over there, I see you and I understand, no rather, I know. Don't be afraid, I will not forget, I am strong now thanks to you, I am complete. I am ready, I am ready.

At that moment I love him the most, I am proud to be his son, proud of sharing that same blood that was being spilled, proud of being more than his son, a friend, a brother, a father, the same man he is: him.

Then the bleeding starts all over again, blood drips into the plastic tube that came out of his stomach; the blood reminded me of tiny snakes sliding along the side of his chin and his shoulder dropping into the bottle. At every breath white and black blood spurts out, spilling over, flooding the bed with life just as life was leaving it. The nurse comes in; his blood pressure is at 40; it is impossible to stay alive for more than one hour under those conditions.

Saturday

Everyone is present and he is as well. Every breath taken in generates excruciating pain and every breath out is a gush of blood; but where does all that blood come from?

There isn't a single inch of his face without pain on it; he's full of uncoordinated gestures, his bloated stomach sinks again and lifts up at the same rhythm as the blood flow and his damn heart is still there holding up. The professors from the medical college come in to observe this exceptional case.

His blood pressure becomes impossible to measure: it's less than three and his heart is still holding up. The creases have now disappeared from his face, he looks smooth but every hiccup is a cry of pain answered by the quiet breathing of the man who is in the bed next to his. His sad look has changed into a mask of suffering, his arm is moving in search of something he can't find, and from time to time he half opens his eyes to look at something he can't see. It's three in the afternoon.

And his heart is still holding, as regular as a machine. Tic tac, tic, tac, pompom, pompom, pompom, pompompompompompom, pom, pom, pompom, pompom, pom, pom, pompom, pom. It is now midnight and blood is still flowing through the plastic; his hands have become cold and he continues to cry.

At one o'clock "they" decide to go home; the messiah has declared: "It won't happen tonight, I know it." Amen!

That's when I burst out laughing because I had the sudden thought of killing him while they were gone, to stab him to death or choke him with his pillow.

Let him die! At last!

Suddenly, while the others were babbling, he stops moaning, he looks better, more peaceful. And then I don't understand anything; the messiah is praying in Hebrew very quickly without catching his breath; he just died, like that without saying anything, without warning anyone... He has just died, tears penetrate into me like knives, I bite my fingers in order not to scream, I feel physical pain, everything is turning, my eyes see nothing except for his wide open eyes that are locked on me in pain, I'm shaken by sobs and shivers, tears flow, my hands tremble, my knees give way, he is dead, my father.

In the commotion the messiah asks for a mirror and holds it close to his mouth to make sure:

"YES. He's dead, I don't see any breath."

He's dead, dead.

The messiah turns to me and with a pompous and almost professional attitude asks me to close his eyes as my father had requested. My fingers touch his eyes softly, it feels as though they will sink into his eyeballs, everything is flabby, strangely flabby, he's flabby, I'm flabby, the others are flabby, the room is flabby, the air is flabby. Everything is flabby. That's what death is like.

Now I'll work at erasing the past. I have to start over and be born a third time! I'm still very young, my whole life is in front of me, the world is mine, I'm in Paris, I have an education, I can walk, I'm handsome. I'm going to work on my acting career, forget about past sorrows, forget... forget everything. Forget Tunis, forget my legs, forget Fabien, forget the sorrow, the physical suffering, the fear and humiliation, forget who I am...

When I thought at the time that such a thing as forgetting was possible…it now sounds so ridiculous, and grotesque! You must not forget, you can't forget, ever, nothing, you must appropriate some things that happen, they must be digested and the chapter must be closed, benefit from your experiences, and go forward and in short become an adult.

But all this has remained inside me, stuck in my throat.

"He'll never make it."

"Yes, he will, you'll see."

"He'll never make it."

"Yes, he will, you'll see."

"He'll never make it, he'll never make it, never, never, never…"

And I will never forget. I have a black book where I write in red the names of the people who have hurt me, who have wronged me, and later I'll remember those who humiliated me, wounded me, covered me with shit, those who sniggered behind my back, those who made me lose all the women I loved, those who doubted me, those who hated me, those who didn't love me well enough. I don't write the names in alphabetical order, they are inscribed as I meet them, chance encounters, chance hatreds.

Marianne's parents have a place of honor among the others on the list; they called me a pimp because I couldn't make any money for one month.

"He's a pimp, he does no work!" says Marianne's mother.

"You are prostituting yourself!" says Marianne's father.

"At least a prostitute gets paid, while you pay him to go to bed. I'll tell him that you used to have a drug addict for a lover and since he's so jealous it'll make him suffer! And he'll get out of your life!" adds Marianne's sweet and generous mother.

Marianne's parents dared say such things while they forced their daughter to pay the premium on a life insurance policy in *their* favor—it's hard to believe, I was the pimp of her body and they were the pimps of her life.

Well! Those dramatic and taunting memories were all very interesting, the anecdotes of hatred, the disgorging of the soul, but this afternoon I must actually do something. I strangely feel something akin to the need to suffer, to recall cruel things and bring them back from the past. To remain inactive drives me out of my mind! What shall I do this afternoon? I'll go sell myself to the companies that dub American movies even though it's the kind of thing that makes me sick. The mediocrity of what I'm required to do is depressing; I have to say in French in a false tough guy tone because the actor I am dubbing is supposed to be a gangster like Robert De Niro or a cowboy like Clint Eastwood. I have to go and humiliate myself for a fee of a few hundred francs.

What good will it do for me to have one or two hundred francs more? I'll be able to buy a pair of corduroy pants for sixty francs or take a girl out to dinner. And then? So what... What will it do for me? Nothing...strictly speaking nothing... I don't want to live just to make a living...

Nicolas has decided to produce a new play and offered me the part of a neurotic. It's the kind of character role that obviously doesn't suit me, as I am the perfect example of mental health. *The Butterfly's Game* is a terrible play by a third-rate Polish writer with absolutely nothing new to offer any audience and I have no desire whatsoever to be in it. But my best friend Jean is part of the cast, which is a major plus, and I don't know how he managed to pull it off, but Nicolas has somehow convinced a famous old actor to also be in the production. Lucien Raimbourg was part of the original cast of a play by Samuel Beckett.

I quickly become very friendly with Raimbourg who has so much to teach us about acting but who also works closely and is still in regular contact with one of my idols, none other than the great Samuel Beckett. I have acted in several of his plays and his work also happens to be the main topic of my doctoral dissertation.

One afternoon after rehearsal, Lucien asks me if I would like to join him the next day for a cup of coffee at the great writer's apartment located just a few streets from the theater where both of us appear in that Polish masterpiece that no one will want to go and see for many good reasons.

I am overjoyed at the thought of meeting the genius, the inventor of the contemporary theater, a towering master of modern literature, a model for my generation, and a great man. The thought keeps me awake all night as I recall every single title of his works that I know by heart, and I repeat out loud the intelligent words I plan to say to him when we meet the next day. I'm ready. I go to sleep early to rest my mind and be fresh and worthy of the incredible moment when I shall be face to face with Samuel Beckett himself!

I meet Lucien Raimbourg at the corner of the boulevard Montparnasse and the boulevard Raspail and we walk down to the Odéon-Mabillon neighborhood in the Latin Quarter where the great man lives. We reach his place at exactly two in the afternoon as agreed and my friend Lucien searches unsuccessfully for the doorbell until he finally decides to discreetly knock three times—what else—directly on the apartment door… After several long minutes the door opens…. The great man is right there facing us, and he appears much more craggy and emaciated than I expected, which I attribute to his age. He's wearing a filthy old greenish bathrobe covered with oily spots and dried up tobacco stains and a worn out pair of grey corduroy pants riddled with holes. He shuffles around in his brown leather slippers that are just about ready to fall apart. He walks round shouldered as he drags his feet and belches at every third step. We enter what he must consider his work space, a rather smallish room cluttered with old newspapers, dirty clothes, open and half-eaten cans of food, dirty dishes everywhere, empty bottles, some empty glasses, and other glasses filled with wine, gin and other indescribable liquids…. I thought I was on the set of one of his plays.

I carefully sit on the extreme edge of his sofa; the great man takes a seat facing us, his hair is as white as snow and his eyes are so intensely blue and shiny that they also appear white to me. He doesn't offer us any coffee, doesn't utter a word to me or even glance in my direction… He speaks nonstop in flawless French to my friend, punctuating his speech with loud fits of belching and guffaws as he discusses the women he fucked, those he would want to fuck, and the fact that he can still get a hard on and keep his erection for a very long time, and of the advantages of bigger tits over smaller ones… My friend Lucien is crimson and can't stop snickering as he appears to derive the greatest pleasure at the wild sexual imaginings of the genius. The great playwright's interesting monolog goes on for a very long time, during which I have not opened my mouth once or uttered a single word, nor have I even been blessed by a passing look… After an entire hour of chuckling and snickering, belching and telling gross anecdotes, the great man's eyes finally shift and descend toward me at last… His white eyes shoot through me for some twenty endless seconds without him saying a single word… Then the great man's eyes move away from me and back to Lucien and, pointing at me with his index finger in a gesture of obvious disgust, he asks:

"Why have you brought this little turd here?"

He immediately rises without looking at either one of us, and turns his back to us to make us understand that the visit is over, and we walk back down the same hallway to the door. He doesn't see us out and remains motionless, standing in the center of his study as if he were in a stupor, probably getting ready to write another masterpiece after that most inspiring moment. As we leave, we quietly shut the door behind us. Our visit with the literary genius is over.

The Polish play closes after a single triumphant week with a grand total of six performances and an audience of no more than two hundred, most of them being older ladies using discounted tickets. I never did see Lucien Raimbourg again after that, and I have learned to forget about Beckett and all the other geniuses, living or dead, and life goes on.

I am exhausting myself in my attempt to become the great actor I deserve to be…Well then I'll go home to bed or just lay down for a while and then we'll see…

I hope that Nicolas will not be there. Nicolas is really beginning to lose it. Yes, I know we're supposed to be friends since we share an apartment in the rue Vavin near Montparnasse, across the street from La Coupole, very chic and fashionable with the Café Select practically next door where we meet all the great future failures and those rejected by success.

Nicolas comes from a good family and is a student in political science. Four times a week he drives a taxi around Paris to make ends meet and pay for his theater classes that he hopes will turn him into a great director.

He often tells me that the conversations he overhears while he's driving the taxi are an invaluable source of important references for his future work as a great director and how those living experiences while he's driving prove that you can have a life of great adventure without ever getting out of your car.

Actually he managed to demonstrate the true extent of the talent and knowledge he acquired while directing the Polish masterpiece that we performed. He spends the rest of his time in the apartment we share and often is nice enough to wait for me for dinner and offer me his usual concoction of rice and mushrooms that has become his daily diet... I understood that he was losing his mind the day he was waiting for me around dinner time but that evening there was neither rice nor mushrooms; he looked much more serious than usual.

He's placed a blackboard in the very center of his bedroom and is waiting for me, sitting in his plastic arm-chair with his pipe stuck in his mouth, wearing a velvet bathrobe and a black beret on his head, his well-bred aristocratic good looks, tall and emaciated, just enough to convince you that life's trifles are of no interest to him. He must think of himself as some kind of Sherlock Holmes.

"Julien, I have to talk to you. Well, this is it... As you know I come from a well-to-do family from the provinces."

I immediately thought I was about to hear the confession of a petty bourgeois from a small town somewhere far away from Paris.

"Nicolas, to tell you the truth I'm a bit tired. You'll have to excuse me; it'll have to wait for another time."

"No, no Julien, sit down. You must listen to me! Well, this is it... My parents are divorced and my father lives alone. He's got lots of money but he's a disgusting miser and doesn't want to share any of it; he hates the idea that I should want to make the theater my profession; no rather, that I am in the theater. Well, this is it... I think he can still last another twenty years and I really don't intend to wait, because knowing him, he's very capable of leaving all his money to charity. Well, this is it… If he dies I can be rich, very rich. Well, this is it… I have an idea…"

He begins drawing something on the blackboard that turns out to be the blueprint of a house. He draws it very quickly and very clearly.

It all takes a few minutes and I remain patiently seated there looking at him without uttering a word. I can see that it's not the first time he's outlining his plan. He must have thought about it, drawn it over and over several times. Every conceivable detail is on the blackboard: the bedrooms, the hallways, the doors. I thought I was in gangster movie where they're getting ready to rob a bank.

"Well, this is it…"—he's so irritating when he constantly repeats "Well, this is it." He must be very nervous—"If you take the 7 p.m. train you'll reach Auxerre, where he lives, at 10:30 p.m.; his house is only a ten-minute walk from the train station on a road that is generally deserted, especially at night. You go to the house; he always goes to sleep at 9 p.m. after taking his pills. He has a dog but I have a way of preventing him from barking. In any case I hate that dog, he poisoned my childhood. You understand what I mean when I say poisoned?

"Well this is it… You'll enter his room from the hall right there that comes from the rear doorway… You see the door right there?"

"You're asking me to enter your father's house while he's asleep and steal whatever he has there?"

Nicolas stops drawing on the blackboard where he happens to be tracing the steps I should take to penetrate into his father's bedroom, turns around and looks at me with a smile. He has a strange look on his face that seems almost without any shape as if it appeared behind a smokescreen.

He looks at me and says:

"He keeps nothing at home, only a few worthless works of art that would be impossible to sell. No it'll take more than just that. Because of his pills he always sleeps very deeply, like a baby, with no fears and no regrets. He's grabbed all of his family's money and feels absolutely no obligations toward me, the bastard! I despise and hate him; he's a worm who is totally useless to society, a turd, filth, an insult to my intelligence. He doesn't deserve to live."

Nicolas says all this without getting excited, without hate or emotion but almost with a smile. He looks at me; I look at him; he's waiting for my answer. He just sat in his armchair with his hands on his knees and his pipe in his mouth.

"But Nicolas, he's your father."

He bursts out laughing, he laughs uncontrollably holding his stomach, and he has a hoarse kind of laughter like a series of hiccups.

"Julien, I never suspected you could be such a petty bourgeois. Really, you'll always be a surprise to me... Yes, he's my father, so what? I owe him my life and then? Must I wait for him to die before I can have my grandparents' money? After all it's my money isn't it? Why should I wait? Let all that money rot in a bank vault? No, no. Imagine all the plays we could produce with all that money."

His logic is iron clad; we can have all of his father's money and produce twelve other Polish masterpieces. I look at him and he goes on:

"Well, this is it then, I could give you a percentage of the inheritance. What do you think?"

I look at him for a few seconds and then leave the room without saying a word. Since then I have been avoiding Nicolas as much as I can.

I decide against going back to the rue Vavin. Nicolas must still be there with his pipe in his mouth, drawing on his blackboard and attempting to convince another petty bourgeois to help him murder his father. He looked at me with unmitigated disgust when I said no, since I had now become another one of his enemies, co-opted by the system, the future employee of some government agency with an iron-clad pension. Therefore no rest today, but more walks through the streets of Paris.

Paris that I know so well by now, my streets, my stores, my cafés, my merchants, my own little world; some of them even wave or nod at me as I go by, but they never really say a word, not even hello.

If Monique calls me I'll hang up on her … I hope old Richard will call so perhaps I can make fun of him, make him hope that something is possible, that I'm thinking of him and would like to see him again and then laugh at him; perhaps I can also make him suffer… An old man with white hair who could be my father and looks like my brother, kneeling in front of me with his head between my legs. That never did happen to me but it must be quite surprising; well not really. It's actually pretty disgusting.

"Dad, let's wrestle!"

"No, not tonight. I'm too tired! But you can lay down next to me if you want."

And he took me in his arms and we took a nap and I believed it was someone else caressing my cheek, who was holding me in his arms; I got a bit scared; and what if it was a different man who would take advantage of me and do things; they say you must be wary, you never know the kind of person you can encounter. Perhaps it's another man who is wearing my father's mask and is taking advantage of me. I'm sure another man is wearing my father's mask, and it is not my father, because I believe I was adopted when I was young. Yes, I know, every child thinks that but in my case I know it's true.

I often looked at pictures of myself when I was younger to see whether I resembled someone in the family but I don't, I don't look like anyone... So? Then I dream sometimes of things I can't repeat to anyone. I often have a wonderful dream I think about:

I'm thirty and I'm walking along a blue beach. I'm no longer limping and actually I never did limp in the past. I'm very good looking and women, all the women, look at me and smile, and I start running very fast and they're all running after me but they can't catch up with me because I'm running on the water, so they remain on the beach yelling and screaming out of frustration.

There are scores of women. Then they take off their clothes and are stark naked and show me their bodies by posing seductively and I ignore them and keep on walking on water without looking back. I walk, I walk, at times I fly using my arms as wings and I look at them from above, from high up in the sky, they are completely naked, and I am still flying and I reach a different land where scores of other naked women are also expecting me. They applaud when I touch the sand, they scream that I'm so beautiful, that I was the one they were waiting for and then they all jump on me as if they want to devour me. I close my eyes and feel great warmth overtaking my entire body, I shiver and I smile. If my Daddy knew what I'm thinking about when we take a nap together he'd be very angry!

Maybe I'll tell him someday; maybe he'll think its fine and he'll also tell me stories about naked women... I read in a book that sex begins at birth, so it's not because I'm unable to walk, I'm a cripple, that I'm not supposed to have any desires. Once, while they were having dinner I found in Dad's dresser under his shirts some pictures of naked women and men touching each other and doing revolting things, so he must have quite a few stories to tell. There were dozens of pictures but I didn't find pictures of Dad and Mom. I must admit that I felt heat and shivers all over my body...

My maid Pina's voice interrupted my pleasure as I was looking at those pictures: "Dinner is served!"

My mother must always bother us just when...

Madam my mother with her beauty, her servants, her lovers, her children, her husband, in that order of importance...her this, her that, her other...

I hate Madam my mother.

When I think that right now she's in the hospital in a public room, alone like a poor woman, and that they all turned away from her, her lovers, her friends, her family,

126

her brother, all of them fearful of having to do something, perhaps even to offer her some help. They just ignore her like they ignore me; we don't exist, we should have, we should, we must disappear, and we represent nothing. They all go on with their mediocre little lives and let my mother go on with hers. She's no longer young, nor so beautiful; she no longer dresses fashionably: she looks like a poor Jewish woman who works as a cleaning lady. She had all of Tunis at her feet. Now she's kneeling at the feet of the whores in the rue St. Denis as she shortens the hems on their skirts for a few francs.

She, who never was a good mother, has now become the mother of all the hookers in the rue Blondel: they confide in her. Those ladies who come from just about everywhere and wind up in the same street have a personal story, always an original and pathetic one to tell. They talk about their childhood, their family, sometimes about their children. They all say they won't be in this business forever, that it's only a passing moment in their lives, a stage, a pit stop so they can finally organize their lives. They tell Mom the complicated stories of their pimps: Yugoslavs, Arabs, Senegalese, or Corsicans. They describe their customers with their habits, their manias, their obsessions, and their perversions in the greatest detail. Mother, who suffers from asthma, must work all day in a smoke-filled miserable little shop with her packs of Marlboro that she's chain smoking and mixes with the smoke of the cigarettes smoked by those half-naked ladies who stop by to purchase sexy dresses and skirts, or request that she shorten the hem but rarely to make it longer…

As they all cough together, the ladies have coffee with Mother, whom they have nicknamed Mami, and relax between customers as they confide their joys and sorrows and Mother, who had always been thoroughly incapable of managing her own life, is now the special counselor and confidante of a bunch of two-bit whores. She works from eleven in the morning to ten at night and then returns to her hovel a few doors down the street near the Porte St. Denis. She lives in two rooms on the sixth floor of a dilapidated building, drinks coffee with milk all evening, smokes nonstop, and eats only canned food. Her only remaining pleasure in life is her poodle Pamela, a big change since she used to hate animals before but now adores this ridiculous little dog and treats it better than she would a child. She feeds it filet mignon that she can't even buy for herself, gives her a bath, brushes her hair, dresses her in winter coats and even in summer clothes and looks at it smiling with happiness.

And I, the unemployed actor, am unable to offer her any kind of help.

Now that her beauty has vanished, that her pride is defeated, that her bad temper is dissolved, she finally needs me, she hangs on to me; without me she has nothing left!

She was never able to defeat me; she was never able to conquer me.

Poor mother, now I look at you, and…. I can't even speak, I'm overwhelmed with remorse, with pain, with emotion, it wasn't your fault, you… you knew nothing.

You had been thrown into life like some kind of beautiful piece of merchandise; you were only a young Jewish-Italian girl from Tunis, with an abusive, alcoholic father who was actually half crazy, a barbarian. He had the gall of having himself called Papi and even tried to impose his madness on Fabien and on me but Dad stopped him immediately.

"Nino this is my house! You shall respect my rules or you will no longer be welcome here."

My father and Papi Nino never spoke again and we practically never saw him but the stories of his extravagant behavior remain in everyone's memory.

Mother, do you remember the cakes he used to throw out the window every Sunday because his wife, your mother, complained that he had bought too many? After three Sundays of that circus all the kids in the neighborhood were waiting outside the window for the rain of cakes and that lasted for several months.

Angelina, my Mami, your mother tried to defend you but couldn't really do anything against the Barbarian. Angelina, my grandmother whose name means little angel in Italian, with her sweet compassionate face where you could read the signs of pain left by her years spent with the Barbarian.

Her face exuded a gentle kind of wisdom and resignation, but also the silent rejection of any compromise. Every other Thursday afternoon Mami Angelina used to come and pick me up at home to take me to the La Royale tea room for cakes. I would go with the greatest pleasure because I enjoy being with my Mami. I love the cream puffs and chocolate éclairs. I even agree to have Pina disguise me in a sailor suit and comb my hair with a part on the side so I look like the little Prince.

And best of all my Mami used to come with a horse-driven cab.

I'm always hoping it will be a white horse. They get me settled into the cab and Mami sits in front of me and we're off. Mami looks at me and smiles. I smile at her, the horse trots off slowly and I can hear the Sicilian coachman whistling between his teeth and from time to time he yells out to stop the horse or drive him on faster. I'm in a stagecoach and look down on the passersby and I'm so proud. Mami is also happy to enjoy a short moment of rest away from Nino, far from the silence she has chosen. Forty years of silence with the barbarian...

But from time to time she says to him in a firm voice that I can still hear:

"Nino, ma basta! Enough! Let your wounds heal. You're not the only one to have suffered; let life take its course; look at the sky in a different way."

My grandfather would listen and calm down for a few minutes; then Nino the barbarian would take over once again. He breaks his own son's arm with a stroke of his cane only because he expressed the desire to accompany him to a soccer game. No one was allowed to say a single word in his presence; he must have thought of himself as Mussolini, that nut case, so then, Mother, no one allowed you to be or to express yourself or give the possibility of becoming a real person? The idea of love had been poisoned in you at birth.

So the beautiful young maiden you were was married off at seventeen to escape the abuser, the soul breaker, the barbarian. Your new family, Dad's family, didn't help you understand life and its ways any better. They were a Tunisian family while you were of Italian origin. A Tunisan family with a multitude of brothers and sisters and a hoard of children. It was a patriarchal system where the grandfather rules with an iron hand in a velvet glove over his family and its affairs… Nothing escapes him; he controls everything but with kindness, wisdom, and understanding, especially when you agree with him. He even keeps watch over the melons and watermelons that he hides under his bed that no one is allowed to approach or even look at… Everyone knows they're there under his bed and waits with undisguised impatience for the great day to come. Finally the whole family, some forty people in all, is present in the big room where we generally celebrate Passover because the great day has arrived. I'm sitting on a big wicker armchair. Papi Isaac arrives as proud as a conquering general; he is wearing his white silk djellabah, used only on special occasions, with a satisfied smile on his face and he carries a huge watermelon draped in a white cloth as if it were a precious child. He places the watermelon on the table, touches it a little, pressing his fingers on the most sensitive parts; he leans carefully over it and finally gets his ear closer to it as if he were hoping for a heartbeat. Finally without averting his eyes he asks for the knife with the mother of pearl handle that they hurry to bring him. With the precision of a surgeon he cuts open a thin long and longitudinal slice of watermelon, puts it in his mouth, and begins eating and chewing on it slowly....

The flies stop buzzing around and land on the furniture near the watermelon; there's not a sound in the room; we're all holding our breath awaiting the verdict... Only my grandmother, who is tired of that circus and must have seen this and other nonsense many times, opens her snuff box and snorts loudly a few times, rolling her eyes, barely able to contain her impatience....

After chewing for one or two minutes my grandfather turns toward us; he has a big smile on his face and we are all relieved because he's happy. He looks at us all for a long time and finally announces solemnly:

"The watermelon is ripe and we can eat it."

Everyone breathes a sigh of relief and starts talking all at once. Papi Isaac now cuts the watermelon in long strips and I must say it is very beautiful with its three colors, green, red, and black. The children run up to ask for a slice, the parents comment on the taste of the cucurbitaceous plant, the older ones are comparing it to the taste of the watermelon from the week or the year before; we're happy, we're all family, we share the same pleasures and we are all watermelon experts.

I look at my mother, who doesn't seem to understand what is going on; my father is sitting in a corner, silent and with other things on his mind.

Poor mother, did you have your place in that strange world? Did you trade the insanity of the Barbarian for the craziness of the watermelon eaters? Poor mother...you knew nothing, you understood nothing, and now you are nothing.

I remember how much I spied on you, I remember… I used to hide under the bed to listen: she is making a phone call, she is calling her lover; I had a hard time getting under her bed; first I had to put down my crutches, then I had to lay on the floor and crawl under the bed pulling and dragging my legs but I'm sure she will call so all this effort will not be wasted; she's going to call Carmelo.

"Hello, Carmelo, is that you, darling?"

Why is she calling him darling? What gives her the right? I should be able to get up and hit her across the face with my crutch, to teach her, to show her that you don't call someone else darling.

And now she's laughing, a big, hearty, and throaty laugh.

What can he be telling her to make her laugh so much? A lot of dirty things, no doubt, I'm sure of it, I know it.

"But of course sweetheart, I'll see you this afternoon, you know that I feel like seeing you."

She feels like seeing him? What for? To act like the pictures I discovered under my Dad's shirts? But this is my mother! No, it can't be possible, she can't be my mother, a mother doesn't do those kinds of dirty things. Does that mean women, all women are like that? They all do dirty things?

Fabien was right when he would say: "We're unlucky, it had to happen to us; look at all the mothers around us; when I get out of school I see all the mothers that are waiting for their kids at the door, but there's never anyone waiting for me; or if she is waiting it's because I've done something wrong. And when I come home she's not there. Charlie's mother gets him a snack and waits for him. Is he lucky!"

My poor brother, he had tears in his eyes when he said that; had he known he was going to die so soon, the whole story would have seemed so silly to him. He'd lived a life without a single scratch and he died; his death was as pathetic as his life. Also without a single scratch, "whiplash," "the rabbit punch"... You fall asleep, just like that, you fall asleep in your car seat on your way to a holiday resort, a friend is driving, a friend you trust implicitly, a friend called Bobby. But then Bobby suddenly goes through a red light at an intersection, a car is coming on the right and it's whiplash, the "rabbit punch"! The smack! The lumbar vertebrae are severed and you're dead.

When I was told the news, I was hoping, I thought, I was absolutely convinced that there had been some mistake, that it had to be his friend Bobby who had died, that there had been a mistake in the paperwork. I wanted that dog Bobby to die so badly, and come to think of it Bobby is a dog's name anyway. Poor Fabien, when I think I was jealous of you, that I hated you and that when you died you were a child, you were my age.

"Yes, yes Carmelo! But of course I'm careful with Julien... Yes, yes I know he's very sensitive... But yes, I know... He'll never know... But why should he hate you...?"

Why do I hate him? As if she could know what hatred really is.

Why? Why do I hate him?

But when I see him next to my father I feel like bursting with rage, with shame, with disgust! So then my father has no balls at all! He knows, he cannot not know and he says nothing; he either doesn't give a damn or he's a coward! No, he just doesn't give a damn, that's it! My father can't be a coward, that's not possible!

When it's close to dinnertime and I see the place setting ready for Carmelo—the name of a jerk if ever there was one—I feel like going under my bed, I feel like hiding, disintegrating, or...or...disappearing into thin air.

I'll have to endure him for another full meal, with that rotten accent of his, those rough manners of a successful laborer; his face resembles Raf Vallone! He does look like Raf Vallone, the bastard! And above all, Carmelo is tall,

"Julien! Julien! Come to the table! But where are you? Julien! Julien! Ju...lien! Ju...lienju ... lien! Ah! There you are at last. You must have become deaf. I've been calling you for one hour; you're doing it on purpose."

Yes, I am doing it on purpose, I don't want to sit with all of you, I don't want to feel ashamed, I don't want to feel my heart sinking. You're not going to ask me once again to perform like a circus dog like the other night in front of your guests. Pina comes and gets me in my wheelchair and takes me to the center of the living room. She has placed a blanket over my legs extended in front of me, to avoid offending the guests with the awful sight of my two shriveled stubs.

"He looks so good!"

"He's just adorable!"

"He looks like he's in great shape!"

"His eyes are truly like burning embers."

"He has his father's forehead!"

"And he has his mother's mouth!"

Fabien is laughing silently in a corner, my mother is pink with pleasure, my father is tapping on the table impatiently and I am all drenched in sweat, I am red in the face, I feel like peeing, or throwing up, I hate all those well-dressed guests.

"Come on, Julien, say something, tell us a story, 'The Three Little Pigs' or 'Mr. Seguin's Goat'; you'll see he has a slight lisp but he's so cute and so sensitive, he recites with such heartfelt emotion, he's a real actor."

"Come on, go ahead, just to please us!"

Soon they'll be offering me candy.

"We'll give you candy!"

There! Exactly as I said!

They all think I'm retarded. "Mr. Seguin's Goat"? Why not "Goldilocks and the Three Bears"? They all forget I'm five years ahead in my class work and I read Shakespeare and Nietzsche, James Joyce, and Jean-Paul Sartre.

"Very well then, but not 'The Three Little Pigs' or 'Mr. Seguin's Goat.' I'll recite whatever I choose!"

My father looks at me and is smiling. Fabien stops laughing and my mother says: "But of course, sweetheart."

I take a deep breath, I put on a deep frown, and I recite the poem by Boris Vian that begins with something like:

"Our father who art in heaven... why don't you please stay there!"

There was total silence, they all look at me disapprovingly; clearly Boris Vian is not among their best-loved poets. So then I smile and add:

"Would you like to hear something else, you shit heads! Something that will amuse you and educate you perhaps? An excerpt from *Mein Kampf*? A passage from *Sodom and Gomorrah?* An erotic poem? A few lines from the Marquis de Sade that I have memorized?"

Huge scandal, amazement on every face, stunned looks, bobbing heads, hands that are shaking, then everyone starts talking all at once to express their troubled feelings. Fabien quickly leaves the room and mother is about to burst into tears; only my father is laughing out loud, choking up with uncontrollable laughter and hilarity.

My dear, my dear father, I spent so many hours waiting for you to return from work, you were the only joy in my desert deprived of love.

As soon as you were ten minutes late, I used to wait on the balcony of our "beautiful big house" crying and imploring the "Good" God to make your car appear at the corner of the street... Tears would flow and when I would finally see your car arriving I would cry out "There's Daddy!" and I would laugh and dry up my tears. I was relieved until the next day at the same hour. From the balcony I see you parking your car in the street, the black Citroën Traction Avant that you loved so much.

You get out with your hat on, look at me smiling from the street and saluting me with your hand at your temple as if to say "Hello, General." It was as if I always felt you were going to disappear forever from my life, suddenly, much too quickly, without excusing yourself, without respecting the accepted rule that a father doesn't die without warning you.

It's now four in the afternoon and the street is filled with people who seem to have lots of things to do and who are pushing each other without any consideration. There's an incredibly thick crowd around the Odéon today! People must really have nothing to do! Everybody complains and nobody does any work; they're all penniless and the stores are always full; they all have their worries; they call them money problems that bunch of bums! Four times a year they only discuss one thing: their vacation. Their vacation, where they are bored to tears, they quarrel, cheat on one another, dream of being elsewhere with other bums that are not part of the family, spend one month pissing each other off and come back to Paris full of extraordinary memories they share with their friends, with their asshole colleagues. Their vacation!

All right, well, enough with the bitter ironic statements; each one has the right to like whatever it is they want to do and to do whatever they like.

Maybe I'm the sick one, the moron, the anti-social denier of life and the world. Maybe it's me, maybe I'm the asshole who doesn't like anything, believes in nothing, who walks around the streets of Paris like a ghost denying everything and despising everyone.

"Julien, is that you?"

"..."

"Julien, is that you?"

"…"

"Julien, it's me!

"…?"

"You don't recognize me? Nicole."

"Yes, yes, of course I do, excuse me, I was thinking of something else."

"I see you haven't changed much, you're always thinking about something else."

"Are you being critical?"

"Not at all, I was just joking, what are doing now? Do you have some time? Can we have a cup of coffee?"

"If you like, what time is it?"

"Five minutes to three."

"I've got about one hour."

I can't really tell her that I have nothing to do.

"I have nothing to do. We can sit there. I like that little cafe. I often go there to dream and wait."

"OK, if you like." But what were you waiting for in that café?

"So Julien, tell me! It's so long that we haven't seen each other. It's must be a whole year."

"Yes, about one year. You look much more attractive, you know."

"Thank you."

"No, no, it's true. I think you have really blossomed."

"You know something? You've also changed; you've become more of a man."

More of a man! More of a man! Just wait and she'll ask me to lunch like my aunt with the laughing thighs. It's always the same thing: you can skip generations, you can skip months and years, but you always repeat the same clichés. Why do I balk so much? I want to meet someone I know to pass the time and now I'm complaining about it.

"Are you still living on that hill of yours?"

"Oh! That's right I haven't told you: it's all over with Jean-Pierre. Now I'm living in a studio around here in the rue St. Sulpice... All alone like a big girl. It's such a cute place. If you like later on we can go there and you can see for yourself."

"We'll see; it depends."

"It depends on what?"

"On you, on me, on what we're going to say or rather not say and if we can still say something."

"I see you're still the same simple person you used to be. I hope you're not still angry with me. You know we met at a time when I wasn't available. I loved Jean-Pierre and I'm the faithful type. I liked you very much but you crowded me and with Jean-Pierre it was quieter. I'm sure you can understand."

I can't remember any of that; neither Jean-Pierre nor our meeting even or her lack of availability. This shitty conversation is boring me. What the hell am I doing here with this silly bitch drinking awful coffee in the middle of the afternoon on a week day that feels strangely like a Sunday after attending mass?

"Julien, you must be thinking about something else. What is it?"

"No, nothing, you can't understand."

"Why don't you come out and say that I'm dumb and that I'm not at the same level as you are."

"How can you imagine that I can be thinking such a thing?"

"Well, all right. Now I know I was wrong. But you were bothering me, you were making me feel uncomfortable in my way of life, the way you lived, your endless silences and your craziness and your reputation and …"

and…

and…

Yeah sure, my ass! The way I live? She would have been better off saying my way of dying, which would have been more original and closer to the truth…

Does she intend to bother me even more by putting my persona on trial? She's seeking explanations for her attitude, she's constructing a whole legend, a storybook romance, a cheap novel, a graphic novelette, a photo novel featuring men who are wearing their shiny hair slicked back just like Sicilians, just like Carmelo.

Her story slowly comes back to me but she should have figured out that I never did give a damn about her and Jean-Pierre and I still don't give a shit about either one of them. I have and have had other problems to tackle, other issues that are infinitely more important than her sexual liaisons and her little suburban romances.

She attempts to prove from A to Z that I was in fact in love with her and that she hadn't wanted me, while that's not at all the case...it's actually so far removed from reality that it makes me laugh or rather smile, she was probably a passing fancy in my life, another girl with whom I spent a few evenings listening to her lofty ideas about relationships between couples and all that stupid stuff until I would finally screw her or she got on her knees in front of me… actually

Actually I remember that she … did give me a blow job in the toilet of the Select Café, while Jean-Pierre, the love of her life, was pontificating with Nicolas on Hindu art.

But it's true that she does look much more beautiful, her mouth is fuller, her eyes now have little creases around them, her tummy looks wider. Actually I think I will go and visit her studio.

"Julien, you know that I never stopped thinking about you. You look good with a mustache; you look like a Tatar. You even look more savage than before."

Now I look like a Tartar; well why not a steak tartare? She's an idiot. I look even more savage! She's really ready for anything and doesn't hesitate to hand out compliments, or indulge in any kind of humiliation. She has only one thought on her mind, and that's to get screwed. She must need it bad and I'm going to be used as a corkscrew for some bottle of cheap local wine.

"You see, Julien, there you go again, you're no longer listening to me."

"On the contrary I'm listening to everything you're saying. I'm drinking in your words; everything you say is so true."

"I can never tell when you're serious and when you're joking."

"But that does have a certain charm don't you think? Well, let's stop talking and go to your place so you can show me your studio."

"Oh! Really? That makes me really happy, you know. So let's go right away."

"If you wish."

"No let me pay for the coffee, my treat. You're my guest to celebrate our reunion."

"Fine, OK, but next time it'll be my turn." She doesn't suspect that there will not be a next time. I can't be wasting my time with loose chicks of her kind.

"OK, let's go… You'll see my home is not that big but I tried to make it look as cozy as possible, a real little love nest. You'll love it."

Shit, so that's what I have to hear now! A little love nest! I feel like laughing and screaming at the same time.

"Julien, are you still in the theater?.... Ah! Now that's a profession I'd have loved to be in as you know my job is not at all that much fun; to listen all day to people who come to complain and tell you how unhappy they are or because their...."

Won't she shut her mouth? She asks questions and doesn't wait for the answers. She's into her job, good for her; at least I don't need to talk that much, it's going to last for one hour at the rate she's going. I can remain silent all the way from the cafe to her place; she's taken my arm and I can feel her breast brushing against me, and that's beginning to get me very excited. She keeps on talking of this and of that, another useless and boring speech.

"What are you thinking?"

"But of course, certainly, that's very good, huh, excellent really."

"The workers are convinced that by going on strike they'll achieve their goals. But that's not the case at all, the issue is completely different; look at the socialist countries…they don't have the same problems, yet they have found solutions or at least try to make changes and instead in this country we…"

Pseudointellectuals have no idea how much they bore me with their shitty ideas. What the hell am I doing in the rue Mabillon anyway with such an idiotic cow who insists on telling me her life story. What the fuck do I care about the fucking socialist countries, about Karl Marx, the workers, building skyscrapers, the fact that Paris is being disfigured, the Vietnam war and the nonintervention into the politics of other countries? What do I care about all that? I don't even know who I am. And she talks and talks….

"The French government just gave ten thousand francs to a group, a club, an association of Canadians to set up in Black Africa a small French Canadian Club of people who speak French in front of the little Africans. Don't you think it's great?"

Great? Little Africans who are dying of hunger and don't give a damn about hearing French Canadians speaking French? But they must really not care less about all that and it doesn't interest me one bit.

I'm impatient to get to her place, and caress her maybe, screw her surely, and get the hell out.

"Here we are, this is the place. It's on the fourth floor. I'll go first to show and you the way."

"Yes, please go first. It'll be a much nicer view to watch."

She's really very beautiful, a round ass, two independently moving globes, thin hips, enough to give a hard on to a corpse, as they say… I want to touch her ass, all right, let's do it.

"Julien, what are you doing?"

"I'm touching your ass, mmmmmm, it's hard, very hard. I am caressing it."

"You're really crazy! You're impossible! I don't know anyone else like you. You're one of a kind."

Ah! Ah! One of a kind! If she only knew! She really hasn't the faintest bit of imagination but I forgive her. A woman with an ass like hers must be forgiven everything and is forgiven everything.

Phew!

At last we made it upstairs but you're not out of breath; are you still doing your exercises?"

"Yes, always. I want to stay in shape!"

"I hope so!" she answers with a hungry smile. "But sit down. Do you want something to drink?"

"Yes, thank you, what do you have?"

"Whiskey, cognac, vodka."

"Whiskey, no water, with some ice."

"Here you are. Excuse me for a minute."

"Are you going to powder your nose?"

"Yes, precisely!"

Good, Nicole leaves the room and disappears into the bathroom. I finally have a few minutes of peace and quiet, far from her and her absurd babbling. I feel like I'm in a high-class brothel when the hooker goes off to wash between two customers.

I sip my whiskey slowly, barely touching the liquid in the glass with my lips and imagine myself as Humphrey Bogart sitting in the only armchair in the room, which I inspect carefully. The room looks like a million other rooms inhabited by single young women in Paris who are, as they say, trying to "get ahead" before they give up and marry a bank clerk.

It's the house of an aging doll with paper flowers, tinsel trinkets, an orange colored bedspread and a green carpet.

The stuffed teddy bear of her childhood on the bed is looking at me with a complicit smile as if to say: I've seen them all.

A little figurine of a ballerina on a round box is resting on the dresser; she looks sad, dances no more; she is tired and rather ashamed of having become a music box.

A mirror that time has deformed reflects my own image, the image of a poor bastard trying to be somebody, a small time gigolo who thinks he's a high-class pimp.

Behind me I can see in the mirror a bad imitation of a Goya painting, a man with his face contorted by a bitter smirk; my face replaces his in the mirror. There! I'm now Goya waiting for the Duchess of Alba. I get out of the armchair and imitate Goya's heavy gait. I can easily imagine myself using a cane. I have the proper references.

I get closer to the mirror and look at myself. I can see Goya in the midst of the war in Spain against Napoleon's armies, columns of refugees are attempting to flee, execution squads in the whiteness of the morning light, and in my head I paint three new masterpieces. I take the ballerina and open the box: a sad little Italian-sounding music filters out; the ballerina doesn't even turn anymore, the poor thing is broken, but the sad music of the box is mixed with the sounds of water coming from the bathroom, the noise of the faucet dripping, the noise of water gushing and splashing over her face....

The music, the music that Pina, my nanny, used to listen to every day some twenty years ago. Now I hear it once more.

Let's go, Julien, it's time for your bath... It's Wednesday and it's seven. The bath once a week is almost worse than taking a nap. Pina gives me my bath, she undresses me, it takes forever, she lifts me and puts me into the water, my lifeless skinny legs float, my little peanut floats, my sac filled with hollow balls floats, I float just like a plastic duck and I'm sweating and I'm red and I feel ashamed. She turns me over on my stomach to wash my back, the soap in my hair is dripping down and burns my eyes, the water is either too hot or too cold; I feel miserable. She pinches my cheeks in a sign of affection and laughs and speaks to me in her Sicilian dialect. I understand nothing. And she talks and talks; from time to time she'll say some French words to make a specific point that is totally unimportant.

I believe she's talking to me about her family who are all coachmen of horse-driven buggies and who left Palermo during the war. They have recreated a little Sicily right here, living just like Arabs in their own Casbah, without running water but with electricity; they go to Mass every Sunday and the husbands are coachmen, the women cook pasta and the girls work as maids in the homes of the Jews whom they despise because they are Jews and fear as their bosses at the same time.

The bath continued until age twelve when one day my peanut got bigger while she was washing my stomach… I looked at it, at my peanut, and I was surprised and almost pleased. I would have liked to get up and show myself in my entire splendor; she turned around to grab a towel or out of modesty and I did attempt to stand up but then fell magnificently on my ass like a wet noodle. She came back toward me and smiled and said looking at it:

"Dio mio! Un vero uomo."

I was feeling proud of being a man and full of shame of being what I was. I could get hard but my legs stayed flabby.

The baths with Pina were over… I washed myself alone as best I could. Rather poorly actually but no one was allowed into the bathroom from then on. I stayed there for hours attempting to do what was required, the most difficult being to reach my feet but I had sworn that never again would anyone see me as a half-man.

Nicole comes out of the bathroom and she must have rubbed perfume all over her body. Now she's wearing a black bathrobe with brightly colored Japanese drawings; she must see herself as a geisha in one of Ishihara Yujiro's old movies. They all do the same thing: it's like a ceremony to go into the bathroom before getting skewered: when you think about it, there's something moving about the need they have to always be so desirable. I wonder what color panties she's wearing, and whether her bra has a flower between each cup? She must have fantastic thighs, full hips and an obedient tongue...

"Well, how do you think I look?"

"Devastating, and on top of it we can have a real conversation; you're really intelligent and we communicate in spirit."

"Please don't make fun."

"I'm not making fun. I was very much interested in your ideas about the workers and the socialist countries; it was truly fascinating, really very interesting."

"Would you like some more whiskey?"

"No thanks. Come sit next to me."

"Julien, I think I missed you a lot and I never realized it. I must have buried the memory I had of you in the bottom of my heart and tried to forget that you existed."

"But I also missed you. Life is very strange. You see someone again after so long and you feel you've always been there."

What am I saying? I had sworn not to use any of those asinine statements.

"You know, life is so strange. When I was with Jean-Pierre I often thought about you, and now you're here next to me. I believe in fate..."

She believes in fate and she dares tell me that? She believes in fate and she has the audacity to throw that right into my face... What about me, did I deserve my fate?

My fucking, shitty fate, so then shut up, don't mention fate. Say anything you want, tell the story of your life, of your sorrows, your successes, your dreams but do not talk about fate.

I hate fate, this fate thing makes me lose my hard on, capish?

I thought about all this without saying it, without a whisper, without a sound, without saying a word, with a pinch in my heart.

She goes on with what is supposed to be an erotic and desirable tone.

"Oh! I love your hands. They're so soft and yet so masculine. Oh, caress me. I want to feel you all over me."

She will not keep quiet; women are unbelievable; they always have the urgent need to talk in every situation, even the most intimate ones. But I made no mistake about the quality of the merchandise: she does look like Juno. Where should I begin? I don't know or rather, I don't know anymore. The solution is that I should have a pre-ordained plan to follow to the letter each time, a little piece of paper I'd keep in my pocket where I'd write exactly what I'm supposed to do with a woman in this kind of situation, when I fuck her, no sorry, I meant when I make love to her…

But why is it called making love? What relationship does it have to love? Is it to justify the animalistic coupling that people of a certain status have decided that it was best to call that act making love? Make…love:

manufacture love? Make as in build? Love...love? I don't get it!

Basically the goal is to satisfy them by screwing them well. ... Well? ... Screwing well? What does that mean? It must mean that we have to be sure they will have an orgasm; women say you shouldn't be selfish, that they need more time than we do, so...

Actually I'm bored to death while she's caressing and kissing me and so I think of other things.

Well let's see, first I'll caress her for a very, very long time! Yes like that... She's moaning very softly, already? She must be pretending...but I want her to be the one to beg me to take her completely... I want her to die with desire, I want her to want it more and again, so that she needs me desperately... She tries to take off her panties, but I want her to keep them on longer... She's almost naked in front of me, she grabs my hand to force me to caress he between her legs...and I am still fully clothed, wearing my boots on the bed... I'm going to get mud everywhere; in any case a little more mud won't bother anyone.

She is kissing my face, her tongue is all wet and she licks my eyes that I close... Her tongue is in my neck, a little pussy cat's tongue, pointed and sticky that leaves traces of her saliva in its wake on me. I keep my eyes closed and I walk in mud, I'm in mud up to my knees and I continue to walk, the mud gets higher and higher still and I'm still walking, I will get there. I'm a prisoner up to my girth and can't go backwards or forwards but I'll get there, the mud is up to my shoulders, I'm going to drown in the mud, in that saliva, that swamp, that quicksand, that they call making love and I'm beginning to choke. I'm overtaken by panic and yet nothing has really begun, so! Let's be calm and collected, I will get there.... I concentrate and make myself think of the blue sea in Carthage when I would swim like a little fish, when I was happy and laughed out loud and slowly the mud melts away, I am succeeding, I control myself, I'm the master of myself and of the game. I'm not in a swamp, I'm making love.

She desperately wants to lower her tiny panties like a little girl who feels like peeing… But not yet.

"I beg you, Julien…let me take it off…"

"No, not right away."

I want to be sure she wants it so bad that it becomes painful… That she wants it so bad that it hurts her down there…that she ends up caressing herself…a bit…not too much, not all the way.

"He'll never make it."

"Yes he will, you'll see."

"Hello, Carmelo, my darling!"

"A mommy isn't someone who gets fucked anymore."

"My father, he has no balls."

"I'm dying of shame, rage and utter disgust!"

"He'll never make it."

I'm going to slip my hand under her bra to find her nipple and play with it.

"Yes, Julien, yes… It's so good."

I'm going to squeeze it gently turn around it and then squeeze it a little harder, then harder and harder.

"Yes, Julien, yes… It's so good."

I continue to play with her nipples mechanically and the words and images crowd each other and invade my mind.

"You know, you're very smart."

"Yes, I know."

"Steak for two."

"Open your mouth, chew, swallow."

"Lend me your silk shirt."

"It's too big for you."

"I should be able to get up and hit him across the face with my cane."

"Again Julien, again, my darling."

She's unhooking her bra and her cheeks are very red and I look at her... The bell tower at the church of St. Sulpice just rang and it's five o'clock and there are certainly a bunch of poor slobs inside kneeling in front of God; they must be praying while others are dying somewhere... Time went by very quickly today, very quickly; in the final analysis that's what I should do every day, pick up a girl, go to her place and make love to her, it helps make the hours tick by.

Nicole has beautiful breasts. I caress them and think they're almost as beautiful as those I would see when she would undress in the bathroom, as I was hiding under the bed...in her room in the beach house...

Every summer we spend three months in the house in Carthage, the great yearly expedition There are only fourteen kilometers from Tunis to Carthage...and that short distance requires weeks of preparation; all the furniture in Tunis is covered with white sheets; we have to be sure not to forget anything and off we go in

Daddy's Citroën. Pina and the other servants will take the train.

I love that house, especially the floors where I will necessarily spend most of my time... The floor is made up of little multicolored tiles in a mosaic that in certain spots tell the story of highlights of the Punic wars. I memorized those mosaics one by one, color upon color. I can imagine Hannibal crossing the Alps with his elephants and his armies on their way to conquer Rome. From my window I can see the sea that is so blue that it hurts my eyes, with the small Carthaginian ships in the distance and the slaves that are rowing and rowing.

...I have been waiting hiding for an eternity under the bed, one of my favorite spots, where I count and recount the mosaics, and finally the door opens...she just got out of the shower and takes her clothes off in front of the mirror, she's only wearing tiny pink panties and a white see-through bra, I can't see her face; I've never seen breasts before, they are big and heavy like two pink watermelons, and she caresses them with some cream.

I feel like touching my dick and I unbutton my fly. She brushes her hair in front of the mirror and I touch myself and I look at the big titties and I feel like touching them and I'm dying to see her take off her panties and I'm sweating and touching myself. I'm afraid she'll catch me and punish me and...it's good, I know it's bad but it's good...so good... A strange sticky and warm liquid fills my hand and my head is spinning and she takes her panties off and I'm hot, I shake and shiver all over, I love myself. I wrap myself in my own arms, I love her, I want it and I feel good, so good.

I can see St. Sulpice church from the window looking at me with a mocking smile. I have one hand caressing her thighs and her tummy and with the other hand with my fingernails I caress the tips of her nipples, I'm so well trained... I feel her hand coming up against my crotch but I turn around skillfully to avoid it.

Daddy must not find out. And suppose this were actually my father or my brother disguised as a girl? You can never tell. I was always told that you have to be very wary, but if I'm always suspicious of everything. I'll wind up becoming impotent.

"Why, Julien, why?"

"Wait a little longer and it'll get even better."

"But I can't stand it anymore."

"Yes, yes you can."

She begins twisting herself like a worm, she moves her mouth toward me but I give her a finger that she sucks on hungrily, and she sucks it and nibbles it a little and she licks it... Ah! At last she's beginning to touch herself, it never fails, it always ends up the same way.

I'd like to know if the Odeon is still full of people, those clowns who are trying to pass for what they are not.

She is taking care of my finger very well; it looks like this could become interesting... What if I just left right now, without saying a word, just "Ciao!" "See you soon!" I wonder what her reaction would be? Rage, sadness, fury or despair, distress or relief? Who can tell? In any case it would be entertaining, but the weather is turning bad, I see clouds and I hear rain drumming against the window so I guess I'll stay where I am and just make love, it helps time flow by … I'm bored….but at least I'm not outside in the rain.

"Please, Julien, kiss me, give me your mouth..."

Kiss her, taste the traces leftover by another man on her lips? And in her mouth the bitterness of her entire being? I should have her foul liquids in my mouth, inside me? To think we are "making love" just because two unspeakable orifices such as the mouth exchange their secretions? What the hell does she expect then? Must I tell her that I love her while our tongues are brushing up against one another? I should whisper eternal vows in her ear and murmur sweet things to her? Swear that it's forever and that we shall not leave each other ever? No, no!

I couldn't, there's something revolting in all that. I hear a grating, rasping sound. When she moans she sounds like a goat grazing in the grass

My hand never did leave her thighs and her hips... My other hand is back on her breasts that are now getting harder and resemble Mount Everest… Her breasts were just like Mount Everest…that at least was what a guy I met in a café told me the other day as he bragged about his good fortune with a visiting tourist. The image stayed in my mind… I find the comparison with Mount Everest amusing.

She's caressing herself a bit too much; will she reach the climax, the final moment without me? I will not allow her to think this can happen. Well then, let's do it, I'll take off her panties very softly by slipping them off.

Now I'm going to ride her and go…go…

In those American war movies there are always airplanes and guys saying "Go...go..." and then they jump with their parachutes. Now in modern wars they don't even jump anymore; they just push a button and you see explosions and people dying, women, children, old people and all that... To tell you the truth I couldn't care less. I'm not the type who would walk the streets with a beautiful sign to protest against wars, peace, agreements, disagreements... Masses of people love to protest and go into the streets, march in tight disciplined lines organized by those who set up the rally and scream out slogans, often laughing and having a good time; it's pathetic... I often hear the same words in the cafés or at parties:

"To tell you the truth, I'm the kind of person who hides, but in comfort, hiding in good conscience. I don't feel that any of this concerns me. I'm neither to the right nor the left nor the center. I am myself. I have enough of my own problems, my memories, so that now I am co-opted by society, but I still have an opinion, you know; all those far off wars don't really concern us; they are far away, even though here we still have specific problems with foreigners, illegals, Moslems, all kinds of extremists, the Asians, the Blacks, the Jews, the Arabs— in brief, with just about everyone. And if you also add to all this the tourists who break our balls, especially the Germans, the taxes, the traffic jams, the weeks of paid vacations that the government doesn't want to give us, the minimum wage, the superhighways in need of repair, legalized abortion, back breaking workloads, family, children, Christmas holidays and the gift giving, the garbage strikes, and Sunday soccer on television. Well? We have enough problems; so then the problems of foreign countries with their war, their revolution, their desire to be full-fledged nations, all that bullshit are not our problems at all. We should just let them gobble each other up and then we'll see! It's like those little African kings...we really don't give a shit about their country's health problems, their economic crises, their famines, their under development; they've got to fend for themselves, find their own solutions. We did it didn't we? We had our revolution and we sent the king and all the others to the guillotine...OK?"

There! I have just managed to listen to an average Frenchman, the guy in the bistro comparing tits to Mount Everest and making a speech to impress his silent and admiring buddies who are dazzled by all his knowledge as they drink up their fifth glass of anisette....

I am tempted to become an average Frenchman, a Sunday morning asshole with an opinion about everything and who is convinced he has every right to reconstruct the world in his own way and after his moment of glory at the café will return home and be as silent as a corpse without exchanging a word or even a glance with his wife and children who also have had nothing to say to the asshole for years on end.

Ohhhhhhhhhh! Julien !

But I'm digressing...

Her moaning brings me back to the present situation, which is to make love to... I forgot her name actually... I do have some effect on her after all, such a moan for a pair of panties slipped off is a bit exaggerated; let's have some modesty!

Some control, some mystery, some class, some style.

"Lift your legs so I can take off your panties."

Panties are so clumsy; they always roll around the ankles; but now it's done. Well now, let's go ahead without any further hesitation. My soft and yet virile hand will replace hers.

"Ohhhhhhhh! Julien!"

She's repeating herself, with two *Ohhh*s in two minutes.

"Julien, take off your clothes, I want to feel you, to touch you, to caress you also, I want you, I want your strength, I want your manhood."

These are the lyrical fifteen minutes she can't just say she wants to be fucked, no! She wants my strength! My strength? If she only knew, poor thing! She's twisting more and more... You'll see she's going to climax with my hand...no it would be much too easy... Enough! Enough!

"More! More!"

"You don't want me to get undressed? No?"

"Yes! Yes!"

She's got this bad habit of repeating everything twice; that's really unnerving. OK, off the bed. I take off my shirt I let her gaze at my powerful hairy chest, just a short second, one shouldn't spoil pleasure by giving too much too soon. I take off my cowboy boots, my socks, the socks are a most ridiculous moment and I don't handle too badly, my pants, my underwear... And I then appear in my splendid nudity… I am gigantic, straight, hard, all…and all…

After twenty years of exercises, it would be rather sad if I were not in good shape, or that I did not impress the young women lacking some affection.

One, two, three, four!

"Half a centimeter in four months, that's very good my boy!"

Twenty years to get out of this.

Mr. Muscle-Pau.

My duck walk.

"Everyone can be loved, even you shall be," as Fabien would say.

I feel like having her admire me for hours while not allowing her to touch me. Yes, yes it's me! This good looking well-built guy, yes, yes it's me, the former ugly little cripple who tripped every two feet.

I got all of you, haven't I?

"He'll never make it."

I made it…my body made it.

My first great victory came with an event that can seem pathetic to everyone except me.

I'm playing Horace in Moliere's *The School of Wives*. I am in Pau, a deathly boring town in Southern France… There's absolutely nothing to do… My old buddy Gaston is playing the role of Arnolphe; according to what he says he's a modern sculptor and he scours every garbage can, every abandoned building site to find old bones, old metal, old cans, old this or that. He assembles these discarded pieces by gluing them or fastening them with string, belts, ribbon, or wire and he calls the results a form of sculpture: at least it gives him something to do between rehearsals and the evening performances. One day he sees an ad for the bodybuilding competition for Mr. Muscle City of Pau. Gaston is already over fifty and is way beyond the age where you participate in that kind of contest... But he still has the heart of a child and loves practical jokes. He tells me we should enter the contest and have a few laughs as we adopt muscleman poses on a stage.

I'm going to walk half naked on a stage set up for the occasion. I'm going to exhibit myself to crowd of assholes who will laugh like my neighbors in Tunis when they saw me. I'm going to be humiliated once again. To be humiliated was part of the past, I deserve better than that: I'm an actor.

I answer no; he insists, by attempting to prove that this a good thing for me, like a catharsis, a useful experience, a way of breaking with my years of solitude...he insists and insists and in the end here we are in bathing suits posing like Apollo on the stage, with a dozen other guys who must be spending most of their time in the gym working on building up their muscles and who look like cartoon characters.

Gaston is eliminated in the first round but I make it through the second and third rounds to reach the finals with two other clowns... Gaston is screaming his pleasure and joy, he is applauding loudly, laughs to tears like a child when the winner is announced and is given a trophy and a kiss from Miss Pau. It's me! I won! The horrible stunted child, the one who limps, the ridiculous little cripple is now Mr. Muscle Pau. Nobody understands why tears are rolling down my cheeks, why I look so unhappy. I made it you bunch of greenhorns, and you can't stand it and I say no to you! I say no to everything, to everything because I have defeated you. Now I can refuse everything.

"Julien! How handsome you are. Come, come next to me!"

You want me? Well then, you shall have me. Mr. Muscle Pau is going to be all yours. She's smiling; she looks like the little girl I saw the other day at the carnival in Pigalle: she was sucking on a huge caramel lollipop and she had a big smile and her cheeks were on fire.

I'm so thirsty, I feel like having pineapple juice. When I was on the island of La Réunion, I was drinking pineapple juice five times a day.

But for god's sake, I'm amazed, she's going to direct operations and I must do the same... My head between her legs, I'll go into the deepest part of her, to her greatest intimacy. And then it's the whole symphony.

"Julien, Julien, it's good, it's good, Oh! You're driving me crazy, I can no longer ah … I can no longer… I can't…take me, take, take me please!"

I pretend not to hear her words…and I continue my work, without thinking about anything, without any kind of pleasure, without displeasure either but with no feelings whatsoever…

…Goya looks at me and smiles, and on the other wall I discover the reproduction of a picture of Don Quixote and Sancho Panza. But why is the same identical reproduction in every young woman's studio? That picture is becoming some kind of mania or a trauma of sorts; it has to correspond to some obsession. If I were a psychologist or a modern art critic I'd be able to find an explanation, those people always have something to say.

"Julien, you don't understand, I want it, I want to. I beg you, make me feel like a woman!"

She finally says the great fateful words!

Better and better, or rather worse and worse, psychology in the bedroom.

"Make me feel like a woman!"

Perhaps mother used to say those same words to Carmelo.

I shouldn't think about that or I'll lose my hard on. In any case I can only give in when faced with such insistence. I lay on top of her. She lets out another Ohhhhhhh! The third time in the afternoon, she's repeating herself. Every time I screw a woman I have the feeling that I'm working in a factory, I come and go like a piston, my back follows and I watch the goings on like a bystander watching a train go by... It's five thirty in the afternoon at St. Sulpice church... The walls in the room are covered with cracks, the paint is peeling off, the furniture is chipped, the faucet in the kitchen is running uninterruptedly, everything is fucked out, my piston keeps on doing its job; if I were to do this every day I'd go nuts.

I can't bring myself to pretend that I love her or play the man in love with this woman who is free of any inhibitions...it's something I can't bring myself to do, even if I could, since I specialize in playing romantic lead roles.

Yes… I am playing the leading young lover in the romantic title roles.

The first time I tried that kind of part was to leave its mark on me forever. I'm sharing the dressing room with the other main male role and I have established a good and almost friendly relationship of mutual respect with him…. On opening night we're extremely on edge because someone told us that Jean-Louis Barrault was present in the audience. Jean-Louis Barrault, the hero of the French theater, who played the mime in the movie *Les enfants du paradis*, the director of the Odéon national theater. During the intermission we hear someone knocking softly on the dressing room door. We open and it's Barrault, a skinny little man all wrinkled like an old apple. He smiles and says, "I appreciate the play very much, you're both very much in character. I can see that you have worked hard at it and given it a lot of thought." We smile with pleasure; the great Barrault likes us. Perhaps he might choose us for a part in his prestigious company, and then he adds, without smiling and very seriously, "But I must say that one of you two has also a lot of talent…" He comes up to us and we shake his hand with all the respect he deserves. He closes the door quietly, probably heading back to the audience to listen to the second act and my colleague, who has a much more sophisticated sense of humor than I, laughs aloud, shrugging his shoulders.

I am more in a bad mood and don't laugh.

My colleague will go on and have a great acting career. I keep getting parts in the former colonies, in the "Maisons de la Culture," and a few suburban theaters.

St. Sulpice rings on the quarter hour.... Boredom becomes unbearable; I must think of something else, like.... Something that has nothing to do with her, who still moans like a top that's turning on itself... let's see. a man drowning—no it's the same thing... the slaughter-house where they're cutting the heads of bulls with a single slash of the sword—no it's also the same thing.

The slaughterhouse is a truly fascinating place and I think I have seen the most incredible of them all.

I'm on the island of La Reunion to play the role of Perdican in *On ne badine pas avec l'amour* by Musset and the part of Horace in *The School of Wives* by my master, Molière.

The island of La Réunion, a French island lost in the Indian Ocean, an exotic jewel isolated from the rest of the world, far from everything, a paradise given to man to take advantage of it shamelessly, and I am enjoying myself like a man possessed. I drink in all its exotic charms like a convict with two years left to live or fifteen years to catch up on.

I am living with the other actors in the plays in a huge villa on the beach of St. Denis and the first five days are dedicated to rehearsals during the day and starting at six every evening the party begins... We are screwing every one of the little ladies of the island with their ebony and mahogany bodies, and for the ladies of the French theater, the men of La Réunion with their bronze bodies. We drink white rum from the bottle, swim naked in the Indian Ocean, and basically live like colonizers who think they can do as they please because they are white, they are from the parent country, and on top of everything else they are actors.

We are or rather we act as Greek gods in a conquered land...a bunch of real assholes that fully justify the hatred and the contempt some people could have for what we represent.

Every evening on the beach I barbecue lobsters, which were simply resting peacefully on the boulders and invite me with their heavyset eyes to grab them and eat them.

After five days of that kind of life full of enrichment and surprises where I make my contribution to bringing culture to the colonies I go to sleep around two in the morning like every other night after drinking my bottle of rum and dancing like a jerk with half-naked dolls on the moonlit beach.

I'm awakened by horrible screams that seem to come from outside, the screams of children or women being disemboweled, accompanied by crashing sounds as if the trees were being smashed with power hammers... I snuggle closer to the girl with nipples as sweet as pineapples asleep next to me and I whisper a few worried words. She doesn't wake up; she sleeps happily satisfied after having tasted the love of an important person and she is indifferent both to my fear and the screams.

I muster all the courage I can and finally get up while she turns around and snores. We meet down stairs in the hall—Jean and two or three other actors in the troupe— and even though we can recognize the jitters in each one's eyes we all decide to go and see the reason behind those deadly screams... We go outside in the moonlight, not a breath of wind, the ocean is absolutely calm without a single ripple, the screams of women and children are now more intense and have become intolerable and some in our group don't want to keep moving forward...

Jean and I walk on in the direction of the incessant screaming, wondering how many women and children are being killed. We walk for some twenty minutes on the sand and cross a thicket until we reach a clearing. The screams of women and children that are tearing through the night have now increased with the screams of men talking and calling each other and we think we recognize Creole singing that is hoarse because of the heavy drinking.

Under the white moon, the night is as clear as day, filled with horrible searing sounds.

Jean pulls at my arm and is repeating again and again: "Julien, what is it...what is it..." We get a bit closer....in a corral that is the size of a school yard, surrounded by barbed wire, we can see scores of giant pigs running in every direction as they are being pursued by men armed with machetes and clubs. The pigs are screaming in fear and confusion and once the machetes and clubs beat down on them, they scream and howl in their pain and death... God! They really appear to be suffering like human beings, their voices are human, their screams are human. Blood spurts everywhere and the sound of bones being crushed is deafening; the pigs fall down without a struggle one after the other on their backs or on their sides, crying just like children.... Pools of blood are formed and flow outside the corral where they have dug trenches so that the blood accumulates in large puddles.

Men are running after the animals savagely, mechanically, and when a pig falls they all converge on another one... On an adjoining wall two men are sitting with their legs dangling as they are singing and drinking rum.

From a truck parked next to the corral comes the sound of a radio playing French love songs. I think I can recognize the voice of Edith Piaf as she sings.

Non, rien de rien, non je ne regrette rien...

From time to time one of the men on the wall sings along with Edith. And meanwhile the screams of the pigs that are being massacred go on and on... Wild dogs are assembled all around the corral, barking and lapping up the blood that is constantly overflowing in the channels and growling with pleasure... The hallucinating scene goes on and on. Jean begins to throw up and I grab him by the arm and we walk back.

I wake up the girl with the sweet pineapple breasts who still sleeps and ask her if she knows anything about the massacre. She answers: "Oh, yes, don't worry...it's the slaughterhouse," and goes back to sleep...the slaughterhouse... the slaughterhouse...

"Julien, Julien, I'm coming, I'm coming...it's so good, more, more, make me come some more, I'm going to die, you bastard... You're a bastard, you make me come too much. I never have come as much as with you...."

They all say the same things to the last stallion that mounts them, the last one to speak is always the one who is right, or rather the last one to fuck is right.

Amen!

"Bastard"? I find her language rather rough.

That's the least one can say, she is coming... She is all dripping with tears everywhere, her mascara is running, she looks like a character in a Fellini film where actors wearing white make up cry over their sorrow and misfortune and the tears streak down their cheeks whitened with chalk. They cry just like this bitch who is in tears because I'm fucking her. Oh! But yes, I'm still fucking her, it had escaped my mind almost completely. Well now it's time to change the program.

"Turn around."

"...?"

"Nicole, turn around."

"Yes Julien, anything you want."

Even from the back she is beautiful, suntanned with white lines. I ride her with fervor.

"Yes, Julien yes! Oh! It's so good! I'm going to come again."

She's going to come again...she is! And I'm back on the assembly line. I suppose orgies must be just like that, working on the assembly line. You put in the screws without really knowing what you're doing. I've never been to an orgy because I don't like the company of other assembly line workers. The assembly line...the invention of the petty bourgeois class, of communist exploiters like Lenin, you work on the assembly line, make love on the

assembly line, die on the assembly line while you are in
chains.

To make love to a woman you love—I wonder if that
is really good or whether it's also as boring as the
assembly line. She keeps on moaning and I'm wondering
what the hell I'm doing there on a bed I don't know with
a woman I don't know who is moaning. She's had
enough, she wants me to come now, she wants my seed
she says, she wants my honey, she insists. I'm still hard
but I can't...I can't do it... Nothing wants to explode, the
machine is broken, it refuses and won't give any life on
this death bed; the machine seems to be telling me very
coldly: No! It's not for you!

After almost two hours at work the machine can still
go on but it can't cross the finish line, it can't end
triumphantly... Once again...

I am a great, an extraordinary lover. I can control and
last a long time as hard as a sword but what they don't
know is that the sword can't end in triumph, it cannot...

The Buddhist monks with whom I spent three months
a few years ago would be the first to be surprised. I went
into their temple during one of my trips to Asia, the devil
only knows why they accepted me...

I developed an interest in Buddhist philosophy for a
long time and I hope to find the solution to my problems
thanks to it, answers to my anxieties. But actually for
three months I spend whole hours in contemplating my
navel and looking within my deepest soul for the true
meaning of my self without finding it. But I do learn one
thing that will stay with me forever and will turn me into
a desirable and popular man: that is how to control my

ejaculation. I can reach an orgasm without ejaculating and therefore be in control of myself, of my partners, and I believe of the universe.

No one warned me that I was risking what I am experiencing now: that I can no longer ejaculate at all but can hold an erection for hours without being able to reach the final moment.

And now like a fat, satiated and ruminating cow, she sleeps. She sleeps and I am there wide-awake and dizzy, my eyes are open, my belly is empty and my legs are feeling flabby, my heart is blank and my feet flat.

And Nicole... sleeps, with her nipples dilated, bloated, and hairy; she sleeps quietly while I torture myself, and die quietly. I have known another one like this who after doing it would fall asleep loudly sucking her thumb; she must have been born dissatisfied; another one would smoke three cigarettes in a row just like Lauren Bacall; another would have an ice cold bath like Joan Crawford. Another one would sing West Side Story and the one that wanted me to sing West Side Story; and Mercedes, who would get hungry; and Julie, who would get thirsty; and Eliane, who wanted to go out; and Michele; who wanted to stay home and....I, the extra-ordinary lover, I remain knocked out by emptiness and the impossibility of emptying myself.

He'll never make it, but you'll see, but no, but yes, but no yes, no, no, yes, no, nothing, nothing at all...

I must get out of here and get out fast, very fast, I have to leave... But I watch her sleep and I stay for a long time. I'm fed up with my fucked-up self, my fucking skin. She's now just a woman asleep and I can't leave her all alone; if she wakes up suddenly calling my name and I'm not there it would be horrible. I look at her and she looks like Mother suddenly on her hospital bed.

My mother…is sick in bed and I'm strong, she needs me and if I feel like it I can laugh in her face and just walk away, turn my back on her and she'll scream after me, she'll call out for me and I'll pretend I can't hear. My mother is defeated.

Now it's my turn.

I can recite poems, sing or shut up, pout, scream or make jokes, I can dance in the room in the hospital and even play castanets and she…she remains lying down, motionless, speechless, without moving her lips, a supplicant begging for my presence with her eyes. I am the king, the king of my sick mother… No more servants, no more husband, no more Carmelo, nothing left, but me, only me.

Me and my mother, my mother and I.

Mother, Mother why did you do it, why did you betray my father's love, and my love with another man? Why? But I can't tell her anything, I can't think of anything.

Mother, poor Mother, you're suffering, you're going to die, and I forgive you, I don't hate you anymore, I look at your poor face of what used to be you and I see nothing that was you. If only you knew how much I love you, I think it, I whisper it, I say it to you in a very low voice… I tell you and you smile with happiness as you cried of despair.

"Julien, how could you live with all those years of pent-up hatred? What did I do for you to hate me so much?"

She cries, long tears roll down her face and she once again becomes the mother of my childhood..

"My son, if only you knew how much I suffered when I felt your hatred, your despair and your silence."

"Mother, you suffered and I, I died ten times, so tell me now, tell me everything."

"Your father never really managed to recover. He suffered too much and could never forget what he'd lived through. He was a poor man, sick and unhappy, destroyed by his own life."

"Don't say that. He wasn't a poor man, he did everything for me. He tried everything."

"No, he couldn't, he was incapable of it, the pain had made absent, he was never able to forget, his life was filled with ghosts and horrible visions, he saw destroyers of shadows everywhere and turned me into a hopeless shadow. Perhaps someday you'll understand the truth and shall forgive me and you'll finally be at peace with me and above all with yourself."

"I would rather hold on to my illusions about him, that's all I have left to avoid sinking, to avoid losing myself completely. Leave me with my illusions about him."

"So you still have all these illusions? Fine but I believed that you had let go of illusions, that you preferred to see things clearly, that you wanted to face life. You can't reject life."

"Mother, I never thought you could say such things, I always saw you so absent, so clearly outside life and incapable of acts of courage and unable to think."

"Look, I'm just a Jewish woman from Tunis, from another era; in my day we didn't stand a chance. With an abusive father, a mother just like myself, I resigned myself, I pretended I didn't exist, I accepted and that kind of acceptance is worse than anything. Don't fall in that trap. I just wanted peace and a semblance of happiness. All I wanted was to be a woman who was happy with her husband who would love and respect me.

"Dad didn't love you?"

"I don't know, I don't know…"

"Well, what was it then?"

"He sold me."

"Sold you?"

"Yes sold, he knew about Carmelo."

"What do you mean, he knew?"

"When he went into bankruptcy Carmelo was his only way out, so he sold me for money, but I didn't want that, I didn't want to. Carmelo bought part of the business and me with it."

So then my father had no balls—it can't be, it can't be true.

"Don't judge your father; he was a victim as well, like me, like you, like all of us. It's life that is guilty, not us, not us."

She is crying and I feel one hundred years old. My father was capable of doing something like that. He died like a hero and lived like an empty bag, empty of life and emotion. I'll never have those memories of you again,

I'll never wrestle with you, ever again, I won't ever do anything else, not take naps, or wait on the balcony, I won't become a great actor for you, I won't buy you pistachios, nothing anymore, nothing. I'll dance through the sky like Peter Pan, but not for you. You are a bastard! I'm ashamed for you, I'm ashamed of you, I'm dying of shame, I'm ashamed of being your son, the son of a bastard.

You betrayed me you lied to me...

"Daddy, mother is cheating on you!"

"You must not judge your parents, later on you'll understand."

"I know that you must not judge your parents but mother is cheating on you! She has no right."

"Later on..."

Now I understand, you had sold mother, you're nothing but a garbage pale full of shit! And I hate you, I despise you, you dirtied up what remained, you destroyed my life, I despise your memory now that you have been dead for six years.

No, no it's life that is to blame not him, not us, not us. He was destroyed like I was and even more... He lost his soul, his heart, his courage. No! No! They stole his soul his heart, his courage.... He was castrated, chopped up, emptied of all life, deprived of his humanity... He wasn't anything anymore...life is to be blamed, not him...

She's still asleep and I ask myself all these questions, I remember and I forgive.

I have to get out of this place, I have to flee, I must fly away, I have to disappear, like Rimbaud, become a merchant in guns and slaves… But then I am not Rimbaud; nevertheless I must leave. I'm going to go and seek shelter in a blue and white silk corner; I have to spill my guts somewhere else and drag my legs along with me as I had done twelve years before when they had died on me.

"Dad, I must leave."

"Very well, but you're coming back for dinner?"

"No Dad, I'm leaving, I'm leaving…"

"You're going to the country to one of your friends?"

"No, Dad I'm going away."

"Where are you going?"

"I don't know precisely. I'm leaving."

"Have you thought this through?"

"Yes I must leave, I must. I have been walking for six months now and as I live again I feel that I'm going to die. You understand, you understand."

"You want to go to France? To see your cousins."

"Yes, that's it, my cousins in France."

"You will keep in touch and let me know where you are?"

"Yes, yes."

"I know I can trust you."

"Thank you, thank you."

"Are you leaving because of your mother?"

"No, yes…maybe, now that I have my legs back I have to fly, you understand. It took my twelve years of relentless exercising to finally be able to cross the street without holding on to a helping hand…the kids don't laugh anymore when they see me, I am finally in one single piece…"

"Yes, yes, you'll tell me where you are, promise me?"

"Yes, yes."

"I'll let your mother and brother know that you're leaving. When are you going?"

"Now Dad, now right now."

"You're a man and you are sixteen."

"Yes, sixteen."

"So go then and you'll tell me where you are."

I saw him again on his deathbed. Life is the guilty party, not him... not him... He became the victim of other men, of their cruelty, their madness, he spent twenty years trying to forget but never managed to do so, Dad forgive me for doubting you even for such a short instant.

You didn't have a choice. We'd have all ended up in the street and you tried to protect us, all of us...especially me.

Nicole sighs softly, opens her eyes and looks at me as if she wanted to know something. This is the moment that fills me with fear because she'll want us to share our impressions.

"Julien you know it was fantastic. I hope Jacques won't find out... Oh! Yes it's true. I haven't told you that I'm getting married in two weeks to Jacques. He's marvelous, I'm crazy about him and we have so many plans. We're going to move overseas for two years, he has to go into the military in the foreign cooperation service, he just finished medical school, we decided all this four months ago. The big day is in two weeks and I'm crazy about him."

She turns on her side, wiggles some more and falls into a deep sleep once again. Goya looks at me and is now smiling sardonically.

I've got to get out of here, I've got to go… She sleeps with her mouth open like a satiated child who has just quickly digested two chocolate bars she swallowed in great haste. I get up and she doesn't even move… So now I am officially a whore. Nicole's handbag is still there on the table, next to the ballerina who looks at me without any kind of expression. I see that the paint on her nose has been erased. My hand slips into her bag, opens her wallet and I take whatever bill I can find. I'm hoping it's one hundred francs. The ballerina smiles at me. I leave closing the door behind me without looking back.

The concierge looks at me with an amused and sly expression. I stop in the hall and piss in powerful spurts against the wall to teach her a lesson; it makes me feel better.

"You should be ashamed of yourself you rotten disgusting man!"

I'm disgusting, you are disgusting, we are all disgusting; the church at St. Sulpice is ringing seven o'clock and I am back in the street.

Whatever happened to all my friends? The friends I was so close to and loved so much?

What friends? Which ones? Where are they if not in my own imagination? Is someone saying of me, "Julien is my friend?" If you exist step forward, don't hide… All I hear is … "Julien, nobody knows how to take him, he scares me." But what the hell are they fearful of? I'm doing nothing bad, I don't speak that much, what are they afraid of? They are wrong to be afraid of me, they are wrong.

Only dogs are right, they take a shit on the sidewalk where we are walking, where we live; they literally cover us in shit. Winter is the worst moment, it snows over it and the snow covers all the garbage and they start over and it snows again; the layers accumulate and in the spring the snow melts and the refuse quickly reappears.

Soon, as Lautréamont writes, when we'll all bathe in an ocean of sperm and shit. There's a dog in front of me expelling small darkish nuggets that look as ridiculous as goat turds under the tender and admiring eyes of his master who thinks he's giving a gift to humanity. Every morning we empty our guts of all that is sordid, the sordid accumulations of an entire day, but there's always some of it stuck inside you and it winds up killing you.

People just croak and I don't want to die. I'll find some way to not die even though the sky has been shattered. I'll put that fucking sky back together, I'll stick it together with my sperm and then I'll spit in the face of those who doubt me. But no, let's stay calm and collected, otherwise I'll do something rash or crack up. Calm down, calm down. Good, well I think I just went through a moment of refusal, of violence, so let me be calm. I almost let myself go, I almost screamed in the street and people turned to look at me, to look at that poor bum who was screaming as he walked alone.

They were wondering whether I was crazy or if I had been drunk or… I don't know. I wonder why I'm so angry. After all, I only got what I deserved and on top of it wasn't such a disagreeable moment to fuck a girl all afternoon; it must be everyone's dream, the dream of many men and I'm complaining. I complain about everything and I'm never satisfied. I wander on and complain.

To wander is not such a bad thing; after all, at least I can walk and that's something useful, don't you think?

I'm walking,

I made it. Period…

"Dad, I have to leave."

"Go, my son. Go."

Had I known I wouldn't have left. I escaped the hell of a prison for the other hell of freedom. I spent six years wandering in Paris, London, Istanbul, Madrid, Venice, Moscow, Warsaw, Berlin, Dakar, Tananarive, Djibouti, St. Martin de La Réunion. etc. …

Six years of conditional freedom, conditioned by my upbringing, my taboos, my hang-ups. Six years to get rid of all that; my first woman in a sordid brothel in Seville on a binge with some sailors I had just met, sixteen years old and thirty seconds of pleasure of having a naked woman in my arms who after ten seconds says: "Come on, be quick about it!" while I had dreamed of becoming a romantic poet.

Next! Next!

I wander the streets of Seville, still searching for the worse neighborhoods, the most rotten and shittiest places. I'm proud of myself because with my looks the Spaniards think I'm a gypsy and the kids in the street yell after me "Mira al Gitano." I finally find the most disgusting café in Seville, an unbearable smell of frying, urine, crud and vomit. I am happy. I'll be able to wallow in mud. Seventy-year-old hookers with no teeth, obese and slimy are yakking away without ever catching their breath as they chew on fried calamari while sailors drunk on rotten beer and their accumulated sorrows smile at the world, spitting their rancor with self satisfaction; at the center of the café a rusting zinc urinal crisscrossed with dirty words, without a door for protection, a urinal set up right smack in the center of the place, and I see guys who go one after the other to piss out their vinegar as they snigger. They piss with a kind of joy and everyone laughs and the sordid hookers make sordid jokes about their sordid penises as they look at me and call me Guapo. On the floor there is sawdust to absorb the piss and the vomit that the very thick smoke can't even cover up.

And me, I'm with them and I sing and laugh with my new friends. I feel I'm part of the family and I drink beer and get up to go and piss as I laugh and dance a few steps to the tune of flamenco music.

Travel is the greatest education when you're young. Go my son, go and discover your brothers, your peers, travel is enriching, you'll see so many beautiful things in all the countries you shall visit.

Flamenco... A short time later a group of gypsies, real ones, not cheap imitations like me, asked me to join their life. So here I am, the little Jew from Tunis. I have become a gypsy in the Barrio Cruz in Seville; I share their life for six months, I share their joys and their sorrows and at night I give shows for dumb tourists who come to play at being gypsies for a few hours... They scrape their guitars and dance for hours in smoke-filled cafes and the American girls think they're so lucky and privileged to be there and literally have an orgasm at the idea of being in danger in that subterranean and hidden world.

I pour two-bit cheap red wine, I'm wearing a red scarf around my neck, I adopt a sinister appearance, I keep my jaws perpetually clenched my act is perfectly rehearsed, I am a gypsy of the Barrio Cruz. And I regularly leave this place of debauchery for tourists seeking cheap thrills, in the company of a frustrated and hungry female about to spend the night of her life and who will later have something to tell her girlfriends when she returns to Idaho. I learn how to love the guitar and the long lament of the Flamenco mood, and the sensuous dances of the gypsies... And one day I get tired of that circus and I disappear without a word, without a farewell...

Travel is the greatest education when you're young.

But what youth? My fucked-up youth?

Until what age are we young?

Fifteen years old, twenty years old, thirty, sixty?

I have been an old man since birth, so travel brought me nothing, it just turned me into a first class pain in the ass, a conceited ass who thinks he knows it all.

It's hard at first and then you learn how to survive in every single city of the world, the same intellectuals, the same artists, the same rich; the same poor can be found everywhere but they dress differently and speak a different language. From time to time you run into unusual people or you experience unique moments.

Argun Hackman, for example, who welcomed me in his house in Floria, in the suburbs of Istanbul. Argun, the Turk whom I met in a nightclub and who took me in the early morning to a small village thirty kilometers from Istanbul for an unusual show. The show takes place once a week: a young girl, almost a child actually, copulates with a designated donkey.

She holds on to the donkey's neck from underneath and stays suspended on him; the child says nothing, doesn't cry, doesn't seem to be in pain, the entire village has gathered around, women and children included. Argun looks at it jaded, he's a man of the world... I ask him if this is part of some kind of rite. An initiation rite perhaps? He looks at me and smiles at such monumental naiveté; he shrugs his shoulders and introduces me to his mother, his sisters, his father, then invites me to spend a few days at his house.

Argun is an English professor at the university but thinks he's a painter and an artist. He has covered the inside walls of his house with multicolored faces and impressionist landscapes that vaguely imitate Monet. He explains his painting at length and in great detail and his choice of colors; he wants my opinion but I don't volunteer it, since I know nothing about painting. Later that night, under the influence of hashish, he smashes the walls by hitting them with a pickaxe to erase his paintings as he screams that it cannot even create emotion in a Frenchman...

The next evening he paints another wall and two nights later he's back with his pickaxe obsession and the wall crumbles. After a few nights of this craziness the house is almost destroyed and I pack my bags.

My friend André asks me to accompany him to East Berlin, just to visit the city, he says. What he doesn't tell me is that he's going there to deliver some secret documents to someone—I never found out to whom or why. So here we are suddenly near the Brandenburg Gate... we're walking in the Berlin night, a black and throbbing night, there is no one in the streets when suddenly three men jump out of nowhere and surround both of us. André draws a revolver, a fucking revolver. Where did it come from?

They all begin to run and as they take off. As if to leave some kind of souvenir one of them slashes me in the stomach and it hardly hurts but leaves me with a gash for the next ten years. I used that scar for a very long time to surprise and seduce, as I invented a long story that was much more colorful that what had really happened. The gash was well worth it.

My friend André later became a translator at the UN and had used me as decoy for his James Bond style games. A true friend.

The museums of all those cities of all those countries make me sick with their preserved beauty, their canned talent, their post-card type genius. I'll never return to those halls filled with the vestige of other times that attempt to make all those who are willing to listen that it is man's fate to create beauty... I eat German sausages, Turkish tajin, Italian ravioli, Spanish peppers, shark from Madagascar, Greek souvlaki, peanuts from Djibouti, frogs in the island of La Reunion, crickets in Dakar,

Polish soup, Malagasy zebu meat…this…that….the other….

Walter takes me to a nightclub where I'm delighted to pick up a truly magnificent blonde with a pair of aggressive tits. I brush up against her as we dance as the other merry makers smile wondering no doubt why in the world such a beautiful creature would go with that young jerk. I'm almost in love. I take her to a hotel where I quickly find out that Blondie has a cock that's much bigger than my own and I run away at full speed back to the night club and discover Walter with ten other guys who are bursting with laughter and I join in of course...

I cross the banks of the Volga River in a boat, I take a barge from Brindisi to Igoumenitza, I sleep in the public gardens of Athens. I think I'm Don Quixote in Spain and an ivory trafficker in Djibouti.

Pietro takes me to every transvestite nightclub in Venice, Vladimir shows me the old Cossack encampments, I go bear hunting with Wojciech, I wash dishes in restaurants, serve drinks in bars, I sleep on park benches, in the beds of all the ladies and finally six years later, tired of wandering and travel, I'm back in Paris my home base, my starting point and decide to finish my studies and begin my new calling: I shall be an actor…

And for a few years I use all this to my own sordid ends and people would say about me: He's an exciting young man, he's experienced so many things!

I've become a living encyclopedia: as soon as anyone says anything it's as if they were playing a record entitled: "The Living Encyclopedia" that talks and tells stories with interesting details, and displays his knowledge to smug women and men who are foaming with jealousy.

"Julien, you'll regret it later on; it's not enough to be fun and smart in society. You're still a failure."

"First of all, I'm not pleasant; they say I'm too aggressive."

Travel is enriching so I have been enriched. I have the necessary material so I can recite "Mr. Seguin's Goat" or Hamlet's soliloquy with the necessary emotion. I act, I'm a performer, an actor, and just like all the other actors I wander throughout Paris as I wait for the next gig, which leaves me enough free time to get into literature and more than anything else to rehash my sorrows, my pain, my failures.

Then I come back to reality; I understand that trying to forget by getting drunk on one's experiences is useless, to live by talking about oneself is meaningless; then anguish takes over and I stop talking about my travels forever and then I remain silent, period.

It's been a long day and it's time to go home, maybe to go to bed and try to sleep and leave all those memories aside at least for one single night.

It starts all over again, Odéon, Mabillon, the rue Bonaparte. I walk along the Luxembourg Gardens, I reach the rue Vavin, I'm close to home.

Home...what will I do at home? It's going to be nine o'clock. I'll try to wait for it to be ten and then I'll go back out to try and meet someone I know as I wait impatiently for tomorrow...so that it may all start over once again.

It must not start over again. I can't stand it any longer, something has to happen, something has to happen to me, the wheel of fortune must turn, they always say it does; after seven years of hunger come seven years of plenty, the wheel turns but if doesn't turn for me I'll take off once more for Timbuktu or Tananarive or Poughkeepsie.

There's nobody in the apartment to wait for me and thankfully Nicolas isn't there either; he must be driving his taxi as he goes on searching for the man who'll agree to murder his father.

When I get there the apartment is always empty, but the cat is there, the one Catherine gave me. It's the little kitty of the old cat we had together. She gave it to me as a souvenir. In memory of what?

Of her?

Of our passionate love?

The cat is meowing and runs in every direction, then hides under the bed. He knows I hate him. I feel like strangling that cat. The whole world ignores me, pushes me aside so I'm going to take my revenge on the cat; I run after him with a towel; I try to beat him, but he's hiding under the furniture and I can't reach him, what a despicable animal he is. I finally corner him and get closer, slowly looking at him straight in the eyes. He looks at me with the same kind of hatred, and suddenly shows his teeth, wrinkles his eyes, arches his back, his crummy whiskers stiffen, he emits a strident kind of sound, and his paw comes at me in a flash, leaving a bloody scratch on my hand.

Shit, even cats think they can do with me as they please. I leave him with his hatred and go into the bathroom to clean the wound. I walk through the long hallway muttering insults at the cat and insults at the world.

He'll never make it, but yes, you'll see.

I'm either crazy or I'm a genius.

I'll write a book and once it's published I'll commit suicide.

I dress like a bum because I can't dress like a lord and it makes me sick.

I hate all those bastards

To die in a corner made of blue and white silk.

I'll take my revenge but I'll remain simple, very simple.

I'll paste that fucking sky back with my own sperm if it's necessary.

I let the warm water flow over my hand; it burns a little, but wounds must be cleaned, as the wise people I met have often said; I let the hot water flow over my hand, the blood stops, the wound seems to close up slowly. I look into the mirror just above the dirty wash basin and the mirror sends back my image…and in the mirror where I look at these twenty-seven years a corner of blue sky makes its appearance. I hear my grandmother's voice talking to the Barbarian:

"Let your wounds heal; you're not the only one who has suffered; let life take its course; look at the sky in a different way."

Yes the sky was shattered but…it's now high time to look at the sky in a different way.